Forty Cal

The Legend of BlackJack

Created and written by Zeek Lyons

CONTENTS

INTRODUCTION

The legend of Blackjack is about trials and tribulations of a real hustler who doesn't have a hundred bricks, a Maybach or a million dollars. He lives in the projects and all he has is his family and his balls as he is forced to move from one neighborhood to another. He must re-establish himself as the powers that be try to stop him. Dive into this never told before story of how life really is. In real life it's not always peaches and cream and neither is this book. Forty Cal is a riveting, raw, and uncut novel. It's funny, witty, and as authentic as they come. It is a must read.

Warning: This book is for mature audiences only, it contains, sex, violence, graphical content, and strong language

CHAPTER 1

It all started back in nineteen eighty-nine with a brother named Blackjack. Blackjack was the neighborhood hustler and he lived on twenty second and Greenwitch Street in South Philadelphia, between Dickerson and Tasker. Blackjack was nobody to fuck with, he had a sharp set of hands and carried two custom-made forty caliber weapons named Norm and Norma. Most people love Blackjack, but there were a few haters that didn't. If you knew him it was all good, but if you were his enemy, he was your worst fucking nightmare. B stood six foot two inches tall, was a solid two hundred ten pounds, dark chocolate and as smooth as a mother fucker….and believe me, he truly didn't give a fuck.

As Blackjack walked down the block on his way to his house everybody gave him dap and showed him love. As he entered his house, he could smell his dinner cooking but did not see his wife. He called out "Baby where are you at?" she quickly yelled down the steps "I'm in the bathroom! I will be down in a second!" Blackjack and his wife had been together for over 10 years. Her real name was Tina, but everybody called her Mom Parker. They met at a modeling agency, and he really didn't think she would give him the time of day. He was just trying his luck, but little did he know… tall, dark, and handsome hustler was right up her alley!

Jack knew she was the one, so the first time he has sex with her... he knocked her up. He knew just what he was doing too, they had a little boy and named him Kobe Parker. Even though his name was Kobe nobody called him that, everyone called him Pooh Bear. Blackjack went into the kitchen to grab a beer. Tina finally came down the steps, Blackjack turned around to say something, but the words just got stuck. As he looked at his beautiful, thick, stallion standing in front of him he reveled in the fact that she was all his. She was five foot nine inches tall, had caramel brown skin, looked like Jennifer Lopez but had a body like Tyra Banks. She cracked a smile. "Why are you looking at me like that?" She asked Jack. He replied, "After all these years, you still get my dick harder than a motherfucker!" Tina blushed hard, "Is that so? Let me see your dick then daddy." She said slowly, licking her full lips. She had been thinking about that dick all day and was already wet from daydreaming. Blackjack was at attention immediately and placed his dick right in her face. Tina looked at that thick, long, black dick with lust in her eyes. Jack whispered, "where is Pooh Bear?" Tina said" He is in his room playing the game." Jack got excited, "Oh really, then come over here and put this dick in your mouth!" he whispered heavily. "I thought you would never ask" Tina said as her eyes glossed in excitement, she walked over and covered his dick with her mouth. As she wrapped her lips around his shaft, her mouth went to work like suction, but with extra sloppy. Jack inhaled deeply; all he could do was close his eyes as his toes curled up in his Prada shoes. It was nothing Jack liked more than getting his dick sucked. Tina had that shit on lock, slobber was everywhere. She was sucking his dick so hard neither one of them heard their neighbor Gina knocking on the door or that she had just walked right in. As the neighbor walked toward the kitchen to announce herself, she could hear "I'm about to come!" as Jack pulled his dick out and started to shoot his hot wet load all over his wife's beautiful face. Gina was in shock but couldn't stop staring. She had stepped to the side so no one would see her. As Jack finished, there was cum everywhere. Tina had it all in her hair and her face was completely covered. As she and Jack locked eyes Tina put his dick back in her mouth and cleaned it up. Gina thought to herself "Damn Mom Parker is a real-life freak" With her pussy soaking wet she tiptoed away so Jack and Tina didn't know she was there. "Damn, I need a man!" she whispered again. Mom Parker went upstairs to get cleaned up and she peeked in Pooh Bears room. "Your dad is home baby." Pooh Bear got up, and ran downstairs excitingly "Hey dad how about hitting your young bull up with some bread?" Blackjack just laughed and said "Youngin you need a job!" He went into his pocket anyway and gave his son some money. "Thanks dad!" Pooh Bear yelled then he ran back upstairs. Mom Parker came back downstairs shaking her head. She said, "Jack you better stop spoiling that boy, he is going to grow up and be rotten!" Jack replied proudly, "Don't worry when the time is right, I will teach my son how to be a man." His face changed to disgusted as a new thought entered his mind. "By the way, did you call that shitty ass landlord to come and fix the hole in the roof?" Jack asked. "Yes, I have been calling him all week, he only seems to answer when it's time to pay the rent." This shit made Jack mad as hell. "Tina calls that son of a bitch right now!" Jack bellowed. As Mom Parker reached for the phone, they heard a loud BOOM upstairs and soon after, the sound of Pooh Bear crying. They both rushed up stairs and into the bathroom. They found Pooh Bear laying on the floor, he was covered in sheet rocked two by fours and bricks. A huge part of the roof had caved in on him. The landlord was supposed to be fixing the hole in the roof for the last two months. Jack noticed blood on the floor and looked at his son. One of the bricks must have hit him in the head because there was a gash and blood was pouring from it. Jack called 9-1-1 and the paramedics rushed Pooh Bear to Children's Hospital. After six hours of being in the hospital the doctors told Jack and mom Parker that Pooh bear would be okay. They gave him six stitches and his CAT scan was normal. "I will be discharging him in a half an hour" the doctor reassured them. Relieved that his son was okay, Jack stepped into the hallway to call the landlord. His calls went unanswered. The landlord messaging service picked up; Jack decided to leave a message. "This is Jack and Tina; we want to pay you next month's rent early." Jack hung up and two minutes later his phone was ringing. It was the landlord. Jack said "Hello" in a calm voice, playing it off. Once he realized it was really him on the phone he started to go off. You could see the veins in his face and forehead as he tore this landlord a new asshole. Both the doctors and nurses both told Jack he had to keep it down. He paid them no attention, especially when the landlord suggested that Pooh Bear must have been messing with the hole in the ceiling and then hung up on him. When Jack and his family got back to the house, he told Tina he would be right back. Jack walked across the street to the neighbor's house and knocked on the door. The neighbor looked out the window and saw it was Jack, she hurried upstairs to see if her gradmother was still asleep, and she was. Then she ran back downstairs, Jack was knocking again. She yelled out, "Who is it?" She knew damn well who it was. "It's me, your neighbor Jack, I was wondering if your grandmother could do me a favor" Jack yell back through the door. "What? I can't hear you!" the neighbor replied. Even though she knew exactly what he said. She continued talking through the door, "Come in so I can hear you." Jack opened the door and came in; he couldn't believe his eyes. His neighbor was sitting on the couch with her pants pulled downplaying with her pussy. Jack turned around to leave. As he was walking out the door it dawned on him, "That's right this bitch is 22" he whispered to himself. He turned right back around and started walking towards her with his Dick sticking out like a flagpole. She was still rubbing her pussy back and forth; she was dripping wet and had soaked cushions she was sitting on. Jack wasted no time, he laid on top of her and rammed his dick right into her wet tight pussy, five minutes later he pulled his dick out and came all over her stomach and chest. She let out a slight scream and her grandmother yelled down the steps "Is everything okay down there?"

Gina got up from under Jack quickly, "Yes Nana, it's just our neighbor Jack, he needs us to do him a favor." She spoke. "Okay, anything for you Jack," Ms. Hattie replied. Jack explained to Gina's grandmother what had happened and how he was hoping she could let Tina and Pooh Bear stay there for a week or two, until he found his family a place to stay. Ms. Hattie told him yes and Jack returned home being able to give Tina good news. Tina was so grateful she just smiled as she packed clothes for, she and her son. The next day, Ms. Hattie was telling Tina about an emergency

4

housing line she could call, and they would help her find a place to stay. She called them the next morning to explain everything. The assistant took her information right over the phone and assured her they would contact her within a few days. Later, that afternoon, Jack showed up with a 50-pound bag of dog food. "What the hell is that for?" She asked. Jack smirked at her, "This here is a part of my plan, I am about to get a little payback on our shitty ass landlord." Jack grabbed the dog food and walk out the door, all you heard was dogs barking. Mom Parker went to the window, "What is this fool up to?" She moved the curtain back and saw Jack take 10 stray dogs into their house. She shook her head. Blackjack had a plan, and it was dirty, real dirty, but so was the landlord. Jack put three dogs on each floor, and four in the basement. For the next two weeks, Jack came by and fed the dogs three times a day. He planned to get the maximum shit out of them. On the 14th day, Mom Parker got her phone call that she had been waiting for, they had found her a house. The house was in Tasker projects.

Tina called Jack to give him the good news. Jack knew that now was the time for him to put the finishing touches on his plan. Jack went to their house and release all the stray dogs back out into the streets. The house smelled foul; it was so much shit in the house that you would have needed a dump truck to clean it out. Jack called the landlord, he told him the keys and the money were in the mailbox. The keys were in there, but it sure the fuck wasn't no money!

FORTY CAL

CHAPTER 2

B lackjack and his family moved into 1602 Morris Street. It was in the projects, right across the street from Lanier Park a.k.a white boy park. They had been living around there for about a month and a half now. All they saw was Tasker fighting the white boys every day. Blackjack still felt a little out of place being in a new hood. Nobody knew who he was, and he wasn't used to that. But one thing was for sure, they would soon find out! Pooh Bear was starting to get used to his new home, but Mom Parker was not so happy. She didn't know anyone, and she could see that Tasker Homes was a dangerous place for her son to be. She only let him play out front and nowhere else. Pooh Bear and the other kids had started a kickball game, Mom Parker was sitting on the steps enjoying a drink and watching them play. Sometime later, the house phone rung and she got up to go answer it. She was so busy running her mouth on the phone it took her a minute to notice the kids wasn't playing kickball anymore. A big man on a bike had the ball in his hands. He had to be like eighteen or nineteen years old. Before Mom Parker had a chance to say anything, she heard Pooh Bear's new friend Big Zeke speak. "Give us back the ball yo!" Zeke had bellowed. Now Big Zeke was the first little boy Pooh Bear met when he moved on the block, but he was anything but little. Although he was only twelve, the boy was huge! He had big hands, big feet, you name it!

The boy on the bike just kept laughing. Big Zeke walked over to him, "I'm only gonna tell you one more time, give us our ball back yo!" As a tear rolled down his face, the boy laughed again, teasing him, "Look at the little baby cryi-" There was a loud crack, Big Zeke punched the boy right in his face, knocking him straight the fuck out. The boy fell off the bike and hit the ground. The other kids started laughing and Pooh Bear took the ball back. The boys walked away, and all mom Parker could do was shake her head. "What are they feeding these kids today?" From that day on Pooh Bear and Big Zeke were inseparable. They hung together and played together every day until Big Zeke moved away. Before moving away Zeke promised Pooh Bear he would return.

Blackjack walked back into the house; he could see that his wife was terribly upset. He asked her "Baby what is the matter?" Tina started to cry, "We need to talk babe." She opened the safe and showed Blackjack that they only had $150 left to their name. "We need food, the rent is due, and school is about to start." she sobbed. Jack couldn't believe that he had let his stash get that low. He was pissed at himself. He took the money and knew exactly what to do with it, go hustle. He went upstairs and grabbed Norm and Norma. They were like credit cards, he never left without them. Blackjack stood on 29th and Morris Street waiting on the twenty-nine buses. He knew he could go hustle down in his old stomping grounds. As he waited, he heard a lot of laughter and shit talking behind him. He looked back and could see through the gate that there was a dice game going on. His bus still had not come and the urge to go over there was killing him, so he decided to go.

There was a hole in the side of the gate. Jack walked through it to get inside where the dice game was. As he looked up at the plack on the wall, it said, "Pierce Drive" Jack passed two girls sitting on the step and spoke to them. The girls smiled and waved back. Cheryl and Lisa were their names. "Who the fuck is that fine ass black nigga right there?" Cherly asked. "I don't know, he must be new around here." Her sister Lisa replied. "Fuck girl, please dont let this motherfucker have no woman" Cheryl said jokingly. "And…if he does, what does that mean?" Lisa laughed. "Not a damn thing." Cheryl snorted and they both laughed, As Blackjack approach the game he just stood there, he watched the nigga with the dice shoot and talk shit. Gutter Man didn't miss any numbers. He hit his number, he rolled the dice again and got another number. This time his number was eight. It was an easy number to hit, so he bet $25 around the board. Everybody took bets except Blackjack. Gutter Man called out "Yo homie, are you betting?" Blackjack shook his head and said "Nah, I'm just watching." Gutter Man looked in bewilderment "What kind of nigga comes to a dice game and don't do any type of betting?" Blackjack felt a little bit disrespected, but this clown was right…

"Okay playa, if you insist" he said, dropping his money to the ground. It only took four rolls and Gutter Man hit his number. He kept laughing and collecting his money. He rolled again and got another number. "Hey homie, you wanna try another bet?" Jack said no, "I will only bet again when I get on the dice." Gutter Man laughed, dropped the dice and said "Be my guest homie." Blackjack picked the dice up and went to work. He hit his first three numbers on his first three rolls. As he hit his third number, one of the guys in the crowd watched and said to himself, "Man, this nigga is smooth, I ain't never seen anyone sling those bones like that. Rudy Ray, you better bet with this nigga, this boy is bad." Jack rolled again and got his next number. Rudy Ray went all in on him. "I got five hundred on the shooter." Gutter Man laughed and called his bet. Just two rolls later, Gutter Man was mad as a motherfucker and Rudy Ray was picking his money up. By the time the dice game was over, Blackjack was relieved to be bringing some money home to his family. As he walked away, counting is money, he was happy to see he had made almost $1000. He was about to leave when Gutter Man hollered out," Yo fam, bring that money back with you tomorrow, we play around here every day at the same time." Blackjack just smirked, then he did to himself "Okay sucka, be careful what you ask for, you idiot."

The next morning Blackjack and Mom Parker went shopping. They bought food, went school shopping, and paid some bills. Mom Parker was happy; all they were missing was a car. Blackjack spent the rest of the day with his family, the dice game had to wait. As the wee hours of the morning hit, Blackjack got a call, somebody needed him to catch some wreck and it paid ten grand. The dice game went on as it always did. Rudy Ray was looking for mister smooth to come walking through the gate, but it never happened. Meanwhile for the next six days Blackjack stalked his prey. He watched his every move, waiting for him to play himself, and get court slippin.' Blackjack couldn't believe how dumb this nigga was. He was out on 18th and Dickerson Street shooting dice in broad daylight, knowing he was a dead man. It just was not this nigga day. Blackjack got out of a stolen nova with Norm and Norma in both hands, then he slowly walked over to the dice game. As he approached his mark everybody got quiet except for the nigga shooting the dice. He was talking shit and didn't notice that he was the only one making jokes... but wasn't shit funny. Blackjack walked right up on him; you could see the fire in his eyes. He meant business and the crowd knew it. He tapped on the dead man's right shoulder with Norm in his right hand and as the man turned to look, he blew his brains out with Norma. As the 40-caliber bullet split his fuckin head in half, blackjack just turned and walked away. Now the crowd knew how he put in work, and he knew that no one was ever going to say shit, and they never did.

The next afternoon, Jack was out doing a little shopping down on point breeze Avenue. He picked his son up a couple pair of sneakers and a few things for himself, then he shot up 52nd and market to his man Mohammed's. He bought his wife a used car and of course, Mohammed looked out. He hooked him right on up with tags and everything. He was feeling a little hungry, so he stopped across the street at the breakfast spot and got his grub on.

Mom Parker was tired of looking like a hot mess. So, she took a shower and put on some clothes. She grabbed her sunglasses and walked out the door. Every nigga she passed face was stuck on stupid. She was the thickest thing walking the projects and was as beautiful as they come. Pooh bear ran up to his mother and asked her where she was going. "I am going to the store. Do you want to go?" she asked. "No mom, I want to stay here and play with my friends Ra Ra and Bay boy" he replied. "Okay Pooh Bear now don't be coming home too late" Mom Parker said. As the boys played, Joe hot and Leak came over to play with them, but Joe hot was a bully. He started picking with Pooh bear and Pooh bear was Ignoring him, but he just would not stop. He thought that because he was bigger than Pooh bear, that Pooh bear would fear him. Little did he know, Blackjack taught his boy how to rumble. Joe Hot just kept on talking reckless. None of this was bothering Pooh bear, until Joe hot says something about his mother. "What did you say my man?" Pooh Bear asked. "You heard me, that's why your mom got a big super ass." Pooh bear blew a head gasket. He walked over and smacked the bullshit out of Joe hot, then hit leak with a one two. Joe hot put his hands up but was no match. Pooh bear was hitting him so fast, that Joe hot dropped his hands and ran away crying like the little bitch that he was. Ra Ra and Bay boy was amazed at how good Pooh bear could fight. They both said at the same time, "Wow who taught you how to fight like that?" Pooh bear replied, "My dad." They got excited, "Do you think he could teach us to fight like that?" Pooh bear said, "I don't know, but you can ask him."

Later, Mom Parker returned home from the store. She did not even notice the car Jack had bought her sitting in front of the door. When she pushed the door open, she saw Jack standing in the living room with bags in his hand.

"What you got baby"

Tina knew to ask him what he had, and not where he had been. She knew Jack did not play that shit.

"Oh, I have some sneakers for Pooh bear and some tims for me." She stood looking at him with the sad face, "I see there is nothing here for me." Blackjack just looked at her and laughed. "What is so funny?" Tina asked. "You just walk right past your gift" Tina looked around confused. Then she went to the front door screaming to the top of her lungs as she looked outside. "Jack no you did not, is it yours or mine? Jack threw her the keys, "It is your car baby" she ran and jumped in his arms and kissed his face.

"Thank you, thank you honey. Now you just got to do me one more favor" she said locking eyes with him "Hurt this pussy for me." She whispered. Blackjack smiled and said, "I thought you would never ask."

Later that evening, Blackjack was walking back from the Chinese store on 31st and Tasker. He had four chicken wings, an order of cheese fries, and a mangle mystic. He looked at his watch to see if it was time to shoot dice. He finished his food and headed for the drive, Pierce drive... and sure enough the suckers were out there. Jack started smiling because he knew it was easy money, but he was not the only one smiling, so was Rudy Ray. He knew he was about to get paid. Blackjack walked through the hole in the gate and waved at the same two girls that were sitting there from before. What he did not know was that Cheryl had been looking for him, but he never was around anymore, and it stressed her.

"I don't even know why you mad, you don't even know that nigga," her sister Lisa said.

"Shut up girl, I got a crush on him, and I can't stop thinking about his black sexy ass" Cheryl replied.

Blackjack just stood there as each shooter kept crapping out. Jack looked around the crowd and did not see Gutter Man, but Rudy Ray was there. Blackjack said to himself, "these niggas right here is sweet." He cleared his throat and spoke up "Would y'all mine if I gave it a shot" Rudy Ray laughed, because he knew what time it was. By the time, the dice game was over Blackjack and Rudy Ray had all the money. Jack had walked off, counting his money when he heard Rudy Ray calling his name. Jack turned around and Rudy Ray walked over to him.

"Yo, you nice with them dice dog! What is your name?" he asked.

Jack replied," My name is Blackjack. What is yours?"

Rudy Ray stared at him and said, "I'm Rudy Ray." Both men then shook hands.

"So do you play cards?" Rudy Ray asked.

"No, I only play dice" Blackjack replied.

"So why they call you Blackjack?" Rudy Ray asked.

"I do not know. Maybe because my name is Jack and I am blacker than a motherfucker, I guess." Jack replied, "Why do they call you Rudy Ray?" He laughed. "Well, my aunt told me that my mom had been sleeping with two men at the same time. One name was Rudy, and the other was name Ray. She did not know which one of them was my daddy. So, she named me Rudy Ray. Jack started cracking the fuck up. He thought that was the funniest shit he had ever heard he was laughing so hard that his stomach was hurting. As he leaned over laughing, Rudy Ray could see both forty caliber weapons. One on the right and one on the left. He never seen anything like them before. They were custom-made with extended clips.

Rudy Ray said, "Damn that is some powerful shit you got right there."

Blackjack stop laughing. 'Yes, and you never want to meet either one of them neither. Rudy Ray backed up with his hand raised.

"Whoa, whoa partner, I am not on that type of time. I was just admiring your steel" Jack gave him a vicious stare. Then he burst out laughing and said, "Naw, I'm just fuckin with you."

"How many shots does each clip hold?" Rudy asked.

"Each one holds twenty-one shots" Jack said.

Rudy Ray mind was blown! He put two and two together. "Man, this guy is carrying twenty-one shot clips *and* his name is Blackjack?! Twenty-one Blackjack!" he thought. This nigga must always play to win. Rudy Ray knew at this point; he would rather be this nigga friend than his enemy. Rudy Ray was playing it real smart. So, he and Jack became friends. For the next three weeks they broke the dice game.

CHAPTER 3

M om Parker was preparing dinner. She and Deena sat talking in the kitchen. Deena is Rudy Ray's wife. Mom Parker was happy to finally have somebody to kick it with. Deena was really cool, real down-to-earth, and was a stone-cold fucken freak. She was an Amazon. She stood five foot eleven inches tall, with her sandals on. She was light-skinned with big titties and beautiful long legs; her face reminds you of Adina Howard, only a little younger. Pooh Bear walked into the kitchen and asked his mother was dinner ready. She said, "No boy, and even if it was, you know we have to wait on your daddy." Pooh Bear already knew that; he knew every chance that they got; their family ate dinner together. He was just trying to get himself a piece of chicken. Pooh Bear turned and asked, "Aunt Deena, would you like to play the game with me?" Deena said, "No sweetheart, not today." Pooh Bear went upstairs and called his father. He told him that dinner was ready and that he was starving. Jack told his son to hang in there, that he would be there in a few. A half an hour, later BlackJack and Rudy Ray came through the door, and they all sat and enjoyed dinner.

The next day, mom Parker was washing clothes while she was watching one of her favorite movies— Scarface. Even though she was a knockout, she had a little gangster in her, too. After she finished folding the rest of Pooh Bear's pajamas, her phone rang. She picked it up and said, "Hello."

Deena said, "What's up girl, what are you doing?"

"Nothing much, just washing, and drying Pooh Bear and Jack's clothes."

"Well, when you get a chance, I need you to come by my house."

"Girl, I don't feel like coming over there."

Deena laid a guilt trip on her. "See every time I invite you over, you never want to come, is something wrong with my house?"

Tina could not believe that she just said that. "No Deena, I'm just busy." She really was not. She just wanted to finish watching Scarface. "What is it about?"

Deena said, "It's about Rudy Ray's birthday gift. I want your opinion on it."

"Well does it have to be now?"

Deena said, "Yes, you know the party is tomorrow and I'm already behind."

"Okay I'll be there."

Mom Parker looked out the front door, and it was a nice day, so she said to herself, "I guess a good walk wouldn't hurt." She went to her room and put some clothes on. She put on a pair of tights, her sneakers, and a tank top; combed her hair in a wrap and she was still shitting on the competition. Deena lived in the same drive where the dice game was, but all the way on the other side. Tina didn't feel like walking the long way like she always did, so she looked through the gate to see if BlackJack was at the dice game, but he wasn't. So, she took the shortcut. One thing I could say is that mom Parker knew her place, she knew to never go anywhere near where Jack was hustling. If he were there, she would have had to find another way. Mom Parker cut through the hole in the gate; the niggas

16

looked up, and said, "Damn, who the fuck is that?" then went right back to playing dice, all except Gutter Man. Gutter Man was back around the way, after being released from jail on a DUI. Gutter Man just kept staring at her, then told the fellas he would be right back. See Gutter Man was a real slimeball, he had a reputation for sleeping with other nigga's women, so it didn't matter to him whether she had a man or not; he wanted her, so the hunt was on. Gutter Man ran around the corner and cut down behind a row of project houses so he could catch up with her. As he was walking behind her, he kept saying, "Miss, Miss," but she kept walking, thinking "I know this nigga ain't talking to me," but he was. As he walked up on her, he scared her, and she turned around. He stopped dead in his tracks.

Mom Parker said, "Can I help you?" with a very serious look on her face.

"Calm down, Miss, I just wanted to talk to you. My name is—"

Just as he was about to say his name, she cut him off. "Look dude, I got two questions for you."

Gutter Man smiled, thinking he was about to get some play. "Okay beautiful, what are they?"

"One, are you my son's father?"

"No."

"Two, is your name BlackJack?"

"No."

"Okay then, I don't have any wrap for you." She turned to walk away.

Gutter Man said, "Wait," and grabbed her arm.

That was a mistake, in less than two seconds, mom Parker whipped out her straight razor, and shouted, "Motherfucker, you don't have the right to touch me, and if you touch me again, I'll cut off all your fingers, all but two, and I will only leave those two, so you can wipe your ass, the next time you take a shit."

Gutter Man stood there in shock, he couldn't believe this bitch was talking to him like that, especially in front of everybody. He was pissed but turned on at the same time. She was beautiful and no joke; he had to have her. Gutter Man returned to the dice game, as if nothing had happened, just staring into space. All he could think of was how he just got played, and for the life of him, he couldn't place, or picture who BlackJack was.

The next afternoon, BlackJack and Tina were making love. She never told him what happened the day before, because she knew what would have happened if Jack found out another man had put his hands on her. Jack rolled over after busting his wife's fat pussy up for hours. His dick was limp, and his body was drained, after countless amounts of coming; he had filled her pussy to the limit. He barely had a chance to relax when his cell phone rang. It was Rudy Ray calling to give him the lowdown. There was a bunch of suckers at the dice game, loaded with money, ready to give it away, Rudy said, "Man this game is poppin." BlackJack smiled; he knew it was going to be a good day. He got up to go and take a shower. Mom Parker knew that if Jack got out of bed with her, it had to be about some money. Life was an everyday hustle. She knew what time it was, so she got Jack's clothes ready. She reached in the closet, grabbed him a pair of jeans, and laid them across the bed. She got him some underwear, socks, a fresh T-shirt, his Tims, and laid them out, too. She went in a lockbox and grabbed Norm and Norma, then put them next to his jeans; Norm on the right side; Norma on the left. She took off her rubber gloves, making sure she didn't leave any prints on the twins, then closed the door and went downstairs so her man could get dressed in peace. BlackJack came downstairs. Tina was in the kitchen on the phone just a talking away. Jack blew her a kiss, and said, "Baby I'm out."

BlackJack slid up to the dice game, and nobody even noticed him, but Rudy Ray, then Gutter Man. Gutter Man still had salt in his mouth from the last time Jack hit the dice game and never came back. Gutter Man smiled, then nodded. BlackJack nodded back, but he knew Gutter Man's smile was fake. He knew Gutter Man was a snake, he would hear the hiss in his voice every time he spoke. Gutter Man wanted his money back, so he asked the young boy shooting the dice could he please do him a favor. "Sure, Gutter Man, what's up?"

"Cand you please let the gentleman behind you shoot the dice?"

The young boy turned and looked, and seen who it was. He turned back around facing Gutter Man, and said, "Are you sure about that," with a please don't do it look on his face. Gutter Man just stared at him. The young boy dropped the dice, and moved out of the way, then he yelled, "I got two hundred on the shooter." Jack picked the dice up and worked his magic. Half an hour later, half of the crowd was betting on Jack, that shit wasn't sitting too tight with Gutter Man. He was now losing three times the amount of money since Jack got on the dice. Finally, he crapped out. Rudy Ray was like "good shooting, partner, I'm up like three or four grand." Rudy stepped to the side, and called Deena on his cell phone, and told her to come and get some of that money that he had just won, so that he wouldn't lose it all back. Deena walked up, and told Rudy Ray, she really needed to talk to him. Rudy Ray played it off, and slipped her twenty-five hundred dollars of the money, then stepped back, and kissed her, whispering in her ear, "thank you." Deena walked off, then turned around and said, "Hey BlackJack, is Tina home?" Soon as Deena said his name, Gutter Man turned to see who she was talking to. Jack said "Yes, she is in the house." Gutter Man said to himself, "So this is BlackJack, you got to be fucking kidding me." His body and his soul were filled with envy and jealousy. He reached in his waist and took his gun off of safety; he now wanted Jack out of the way.

When Deena got back to the house, she put the money up, then called Tina, telling her not to forget about Rudy Ray's birthday party, that it would be starting around eight. Rudy Ray didn't know nothing about the party, he thought him and Deena were going out to dinner. She laughed. "Oh, okay…right…I got his dinner, it's right here between my legs."

Mom Parker said, "Girl your ass is nasty."

"Who me? No, not me." Just a giggling. "Bitch please, don't act like Jack don't be licking all over that pussy, and probably that ass, too."

"Girl bye, I'll see your crazy ass at the party."

Meanwhile, back at the dice game, it was Jack's turn to shoot again, all bets were down. Gutter Man was sweating bullets, he had three grand on the ground and he needed Jack to crap out. But Jack showed no mercy, and in two rolls, it was over. Jack, Rudy, and half the crowd was picking up Gutter Man's money. Gutter Man yelled out, "Hold the fuck up, let me see the mother fucken dice, I think this nigga been cheating." He knew Jack wasn't cheating because he was the one who brought the dice to the game. He just needed an excuse for what he was about to do. He picked the dice up like he was checking them to see if they were loaded, and then went to reach. Before he could get his hand under his shirt, BlackJack had Norma pointed right between his eyes. Gutter Man was trying to explain himself, but Jack told him to shut the fuck up, and that he had only five seconds to say a prayer. "One" . . . Jack clicked the hammer back; just as he was about to pull the trigger, the police pulled up, and told Jack to drop his weapon. BlackJack knew he was in a tight spot, the only thing he had going for him was that his back was to the cops, and they could not see his face. Then police backup pulled up and Jack knew it was only a matter of time. The cops repeated it again, this time over the car speakers. "You have ten seconds to turn around, and drop your weapon." BlackJack raised his hands in surrender and acted like he was about to put his gun down on the ground. Then he took off; he ran under the monkey bars, and right into the middle of Pierce Drive. The cops wanted to shoot, but there were children everywhere, so he cut through the basketball game, then jumped over the green poles and headed straight for the brick wall. Everybody knew in the projects, that once you made it over that gate, you would be home free. The police were just too lazy to get out of their cars and hop the gate; plus, it trapped their patrol cars inside the drive. BlackJack headed straight for the gate. The cops were in hot pursuit. He wasn't going back to jail under any circumstances. While running at full speed, he put one foot on the brick wall, and over the fence and wires he went. He was so high in the air, it looked like he was gliding in slow motion. Wow, some real fucken matrix type shit. When he hit the ground, his body went into a full roll.

And when he came up out of that roll, he had Norm and Norma in each hand, ready for whatever. As his adrenaline began to calm down, he realized it was nobody in front of him, so he got up and began to run. He could hear sirens coming from all directions. He felt like they were closing in on him. He thought that he was gonna have to go out in a blaze of glory, until he saw Cheryl telling him to come into her house. While BlackJack sat in Cheryl's house, the police were everywhere. They had the dogs out; the helicopters were flying around; they were knocking on people's doors asking questions. It was almost worse than a faggot searching for his lost bag of dicks.

CHAPTER 4

After about a few hours, BlackJack moved the curtain and peeped out the window. He saw a cop sitting on the corner. Not knowing whether the cops were still looking for him, he knew he couldn't leave and take that chance. Jack walked back over to the couch and sat down. He had a look of disgust on his face, and felt like he was trapped in front of people that he didn't even know. He didn't know what his next move was going to be. "Shit, I might have to kill everybody in this mother fucker." Cheryl looked, seeing Jack was lost in thought; so, she spoke up.

"Jack, is everything okay?"

Jack snapped out of it. "Yes, I'm good, I just want to apologize for any inconvenience—"

"No, no, you good. I am a real good friend of Rudy Ray's, that's why I helped you." Cheryl was lying, she didn't even really know Rudy Ray. She just had a crush on Jack. "Don't worry about it, you can stay here until the coast is clear."

BlackJack was wondering, "Why is this bitch being so nice to me, something must be up," he thought, but he had no choice. The law was on his ass, so he relaxed and checked Norm and Norma to make sure that the safeties were still on. He didn't want no mistakes. If he had to kill both of those bitches, he wanted to know that he meant to do it. He went to use his cell phone and noticed it wasn't on his hip; he must have dropped it hauling ass from the police. BlackJack asked Cheryl if she could do him a favor. She jumped at the chance.

"I dropped my phone; can you see if you can find it for me?"

Cheryl said, "Ok," then handed Jack the house phone. "Here, calls your phone so that I can hear it ringing." Then she left out. Cheryl returned ten minutes later with Jack's phone in her hand. "Here, you must have dropped it when you jumped over that gate, it was laying in the grass."

BlackJack took his phone and thanked her. He had two missed calls, both of them were from his wife, Tina. Jack excused himself and went to the dining room to call her. Although she was worried and scared to, she knew better than to be blowing up his phone. She knew as long as he was still breathing, he would always call her back. Mom Parker was sitting there with her mind racing and her gun loaded, wondering if she was going to have to do something she really didn't want to do, like put a cap in a nigga's ass for doing something to Jack. She put on her vest and tied up her sneakers, then checked her clip and started to pray. In the middle of her prayer, the phone rang. She knew it was Jack.

"Hello, Jack are you okay?"

"Yes honey, I'm fine." Jack told her what really happened and that he needed to lie low.

"Are you safe where you are? Because if you are, then stay there until the coast is clear."

Jack knew Tina always had his back, and he loved her for that. "Have you heard anything from Rudy Ray?"

"No."

"Okay then, when you do, tell him I will call him later."

"Mom Parker hung the phone up and was relieved that her husband was safe. So she called Deena and told her that she would be at the party, but

Jack couldn't make it.

Rudy Ray knew that shit between BlackJack and Gutter Man was far from over. Gutter Man was a sore loser, and he wasn't afraid of bussing his gun. Gutter Man had a few bodies under his belt, which made niggas respect him, but he couldn't be trusted. He was the kind of man that would shake your hand one minute, and then shoot you in your back the next. Rudy Ray didn't give a fuck, though; he was rolling with his man, Jack. Rudy Ray was a humble soul, until you fucked with him, then he would let out the beast within. He was originally from across the tracks, from Twenty-Second and Kimball Street, but he moved out of Tasker as a young teenager. He never really liked handguns, but if you gave him a six-shot-riot-pump, he would act a fucken fool. Rudy Ray checked his watch. It was almost time to take his wife out to dinner, so he thought, anyway. As Deena was putting the finishing touches on his party, Tina and Pooh Bear walked in the door.

"Sorry, I had to bring Pooh Bear with me, there was nobody home to watch him."

"Girl shut up, you said it like it was going to be a problem or something. Pooh Bear, go upstairs, and when the party starts, you stay there."

Rudy Ray called the house to see if Deena was ready to go. She said, "Yes, but how far are you away?

"Not far at all, only about five minutes."

Deena hung up and said, "All shit," and signaled to everybody to get ready. As she ran and turned off all the lights, Rudy Ray was almost at the house. When he got there, he turned the doorknob, but the door was locked. "What the fuck, my door is never locked this time of day." Thinking something was wrong, Rudy Ray put his key in the door, unlocked it, and pushed it open. Calling out Deena's name, there was no answer; everything was so dark he couldn't see anything. So, he ran upstairs bussing his room door open, and all he saw was Pooh Bear sitting on the bed playing the game. He gave Pooh Bear a strange look. "What the fuck is going on here?" Panicking, he ran back downstairs. Then the lights came on and everybody shouted, "Surprise! Rudy Ray, it's your birthday party! Anyway, it's your birthday, now let's party like we in the club." Rudy Ray removed his hand away from his chest and let out a sigh of relief. His family was alright, so he started dancing and enjoying the music.

Back at Cheryl's house, BlackJack, Cheryl, and her sister, Lisa, was sitting in the living room watching movies. Jack heard something upstairs and jumped up. Cheryl said, "Be easy, Jack, it's only my mother, and she never comes downstairs." Jack sat back down, as she moved a little closer, sensing Cheryl was on his dick. He played right along to the song. It started getting late. Lisa had dozed off on the other couch. Jack then remembered, "Oh shit, I almost forgot to call Rudy and wish him a happy birthday." BlackJack called; Rudy Ray answered.

"Happy birthday player player."

"Thanks Jack, are you good?"

"I could be better."

Jack could tell by the noise and the music that the party was jumpin'. Diana Ross' "I Can't Hurry Love" was playing in the background. Rudy Ray told Jack all about the threats and promises Gutter Man was making. BlackJack let it all soak in, he knew exactly what he had to do. Jack put his phone away and noticed that Cheryl was staring at his print between his legs. His dick started getting hard.

"Is there a problem, sweetheart?"

"No, there is no problem. I was just wondering . . ."

"Wondering what?"

"If you wouldn't mind if I suck your dick."

Jack pulled his dick right out. "No, I wouldn't mind at all."

Cheryl was amazed at how long and black this nigga dick was. Jack snapped her right out of thought by hitting her in the face with his dick. "Now, that was cute, but you need to go back over there and sit down, you're not going to be able to take what I'm about to do standing up."

Jack backed up laughing and flopped down on the chair. He then slid out of his pants and put Norm and Norma on each arm of the chair. She got between Jack's legs and down on her knees, and put his dick right in her mouth. He couldn't believe how warm this bitch mouth was. Jack's manhood melted right in her mouth. He felt like he was trapped in a three-alarm fire; she was giving him the best dick suck of his life. When his eyes started rolling up in his head, he knew she was a pro. She then took her tongue and licked all around the head of his dick. That shit made Jack's dick even harder; slob was dripping all down his shaft. She was looking Jack in his eyes — looking so cute and innocent. That shit made Jack's blood boil. So, he grabbed the back of her head and rammed his dick to the back of her mouth. She pushed him away and started to gag. She excused herself. "Wow, I wasn't expecting that." Jack smiled; he loved to see women choking off of his dick. She regained her composure and took Jack's dick in her mouth, all the way down to his balls. Jack could feel his dick halfway down her throat. And she didn't even choke, not once. He couldn't believe she was doing this, without choking, but she was. As she was tightening up her throat, she was pinching on his nipples. That shit was driving Jack wild. "This bitch just took nine and a half inches of dick and made it disappear in her throat. And if this bitch pinches my nipples one more time, I will explode right in her fucken mouth." Two minutes later, she pinched his nipples again; Jack grabbed her by her ears and started cumming all down her throat. His dick was so far in her mouth, he felt like he was busting all over the top of her lungs. Then all of a sudden, she turned it up a notch. The pressure got three times stronger, and she didn't release him until his dick was bone dry. Jack finally opened his eyes, and all he could see was Cheryl's sister, Lisa, sitting on the other couch watching them, playing with her pussy. She came really hard, then lay back down and went back to sleep.

The next morning, Jack woke up well rested and could smell breakfast cooking in the kitchen. Lisa was still asleep, so it must have been Cheryl. He was starting to like her more and more, knowing she was willing to cook. Jack got up and walked into the kitchen. Cheryl gave him a towel, a washcloth, some soap, and some toothpaste with a toothbrush, and told him to go upstairs and clean himself off. Jack headed for the bathroom. Just as he got near the steps, he could see Lisa sleeping with one leg hanging off the couch, and her pussy was wide open. Jack thought about it, but that morning piss that he had to take made him rush up the steps. BlackJack and Cheryl sat in the kitchen having some breakfast. He was really starting to enjoy her company, plus her dick-suck game was first-class.

"So, tells me, Cheryl, how often do you like to suck dick?"

"Shit, all day, every day if I fuck with you like that."

To Jack that was too good to be true. "Okay that is what's up, when are you gonna let me get a shot of that fat pussy that you got?"

Cheryl said, "Never."

Jack said, "What, what do you mean, never?"

"Just what I said. Are you going to marry me?"

Jack just looked at her like, the fuck…she was crazy.

After a long pause, Cheryl said, "I didn't think so, but I will still suck your dick anytime you want me to."

"Now wait a minute, you will suck my dick anytime I want you to, but you won't give me any of that pussy? What kind of shit is that?" Jack wasn't feeling that shit at all.

"Look Jack, I'm a virgin and I am saving myself for my husband! Both my sister and I are, she's is a virgin too"

"You know what, Cheryl, tell that shit to someone who is going to believe you. As a matter of fact, how old are you?" Jack was thinking "if this bitch says something crazy, I will kill her right here at this table." He reached down and clicked the safety off of Norm.

"Well let me see, I'm twenty-three, and my sister is twenty-four."

Jack sighed in relief, then he put the safety back on his gun. "So, let me get this straight, all you do is suck dick?"

"Yes, and all my sister do is get fucked in her ass." Jack was finding this shit hard to believe. "Okay, if you don't believe me, then I will prove it to you." Cheryl stood up and took off her sweatpants and her panties. She then sat on the table right in front of Jack, and cocked her legs wide open. Jack looked at her pretty trimmed pussy, and sure enough, her hymen was still intact.

"But your sister was watching us last night and playing with herself."

Cheryl said, "I know, she always does that, but you can go and check her, too. She won't mind."

Jack got up, went into the living room, walked over to Lisa who was still asleep on the couch, and rolled her over. Lisa opened her eyes, but never said a word. Jack opened her legs as wide as they would go, and he got the same results that he got from Cheryl. Lisa's hymen was still intact, too. Jack sat down in disbelief. He had two virgins in his presence, and he wasn't going to get no pussy because he wasn't marrying neither one of those bitches. To him, they were both still whores. Jack started getting bored sitting around doing nothing, so he decided by nightfall the coasts should be clear; hours and hours had gone by.

It was now after eight pm. Jack peeked out the window and there were no cops in sight. So, he closed the curtain and told Cheryl he was about to leave.

Cheryl said, "No, Jack you can't leave yet."

Jack said, "And why not?" thinking she knew something he didn't.

"Because, you haven't fucked my sister in her ass, yet."

"What, what kind of games are you playing?"

"Jack, I'm not playing any games, every nigga dick that I sucked, they always fucked my sister in her ass."

Jack couldn't believe what he was hearing, but he wasn't about to turn down no ass shot. He got up and walked back into the kitchen. Lisa was standing at the stove cooking her some Oodles of Noodles. Jack positioned himself directly behind her; she kept stirring her noodles as if she didn't know he was standing there. Jack could tell from earlier that morning that Lisa didn't have any panties on, so he pulled his dick out, and popped it right in her ass. She took it all the way in, never even bending over. Jack was wearing that ass out, standing straight the fuck up. Her nipples got really hard as Jack skillfully stroked her butt hole; her nipples were sticking out of her halter top; you could tell she had no bra on. Jack held her by her throat, whispering in her ear, telling her that everything was going to be okay, as he continued to bust her ass wide open; she never made a sound. Jack couldn't hold back any longer. As Cheryl was watching him butt-fuck the shit out of her sister, he pulled Lisa by her hair, then came all up in her ass. That's when she finally closed her eyes and let out a slight moan. Jack pulled his dick out, then washed it off in the kitchen sink. He patted her on her ass and walked out the back door. With come dripping all down the back of her legs, Lisa just reached over and finished stirring her noodles like nothing ever happened.

CHAPTER 5

G utter Man was chillin' at Josephine's house. Josephine was just that—a fiend—and the bitch was dirty as all outdoors. Her house was always clean and up-to-date, but she was old and beat down; her feet and underarms never stunk, but you could smell her ass a mile away. But that's where all the drug money went to. Gutter Man had been there ever since the incident at the dice game. Tthe police had questioned him that day about what went down, but Gutter Man told them he didn't know the guy—it probably was just some weirdo trying to get a lick. Josephine always waited on Gutter Man hand and foot; her house was where he did all his willing and dealing. With his feet up on the coffee table, relaxing, he began to snort his dope. He had two naked freaks on each side of him, and they were snorting dope, too; getting themselves ready for the fuck fest that was about to happen. And the real fucked up part about it is that one of the naked girls on the couch next to him was his right-hand-man's wife.

Now, over at BlackJack's house, he was chillin' in his tub with his eyes closed, getting a much-needed massage from his wife. She was glad that he was home, and so was Pooh Bear. Rudy Ray had told Jack that Gutter Man had kept his mouth shut, and the cops didn't know who he was. Jack was relieved hearing that good news. He had to make some moves, and now was the time. Rudy Ray was around at the dice game and it started getting dark. He felt like leaving because the dice game was really weak. Shit just wasn't the same without Jack. He laid his last back down of the night; the shooter hit his number; that put a smile on Rudy Ray's face, until he tried to collect his money. There were four new guys at the dice game that Rudy Ray didn't know, and they had no plans on paying him. Rudy didn't raise his voice, at all. He just simply said, "Gentlemen, around here, we don't do no ass betting." Two of the men flashed on Rudy, and told him to get the fuck out of there. Rudy Ray tilted his head to the side and just walked off. The four men stayed there talking as if the shit that they just did wasn't out-of-pocket. Five minutes later, all you heard was *boom*, then a chunk of project wall hit the ground . . . *click, click, boom, click, click, boom* . . . Rudy Ray had his six-shot-riot pump and was acting a fool, but the niggas must have been some real killers because all they did was took cover and returned fire.

Meanwhile, BlackJack was making some much needed moves. He had just picked up four street contracts, and was in the middle of a negotiation for a fifth, when his cell phone rang. It was Rudy Ray telling him the position that he was in, and he was badly outnumbered. Jack told him to stay low and to keep firing until he got there. It was just Rudy Ray's luck that Jack was right across the street from where he was; he was on Mountain Drive handling some business; it seemed like Jack wasn't the only one in the projects that wanted Gutter Man dead. Rudy Ray was down to his last shot when he seen a car coming through the drive like a bat out of hell. The four men turned thinking it was the police, but they hadn't seen, nor heard, any sirens. Jack turned the car up to the center of Pierce Drive. He threw the car in neutral and let the car glide to a stop. Then he stepped out with Norm and Norma in each hand, and they were ready to sing like they were both at a rock concert. He reached back into the car and threw it into drive; the car headed in the killer's direction. Then the car hit a pole and the front tires blew out. *boom*. The men jumped, then they hit that car with everything they had. They thought somebody was in the car. When they finished with the car, it had so many holes in it, you would think it was made in Green Bay. They tried to reload, but Jack refused to let them. He let Norm and Norma off of their leashes, and they started howling like wolves do when it is a full moon. Jack had blacked the fuck out, and all you could hear through the air was his theme music— *block ah, block ah, block ah, block block, block ah, block ah, block ah*— BlackJack let all forty-two shots go, twenty-one from each cannon. Even after the clips were empty, Jack was still pulling the triggers with smoke coming from both barrels. Rudy Ray snapped him out of it. "Jack, we have to get out of here, everybody is dead."

Back at Josephine's house, Gutter Man heard what happened the next day. He couldn't believe what he was hearing, the four men that got killed last night were all professionals. Gutter Man had hired them to take out BlackJack. After that, he realized Jack was the real deal and all seriousness began to set in. While Gutter Man was thinking about how much shit he'd just stepped in, Jack and mom Parker were dancing and enjoying each other's company. Mom Parker's favorite song came on the radio, it was Teddy Pendergrass' "Love TKO". Mom Parker ran over to the radio and turned it up really loud. Jack grabbed his wife and started spinning her around singing the song to her. Even though Jack didn't know all the words, he knew his wife loved when he sung to her. Jack started singing, "I think you better let it go, it looks like another love TKO, you take control of my mind, like you are supposed to, you take some bumps, and bruises from a two-time loser, but you got to letting go, looks like another love TKO," Pooh Bear stood on the steps and watched this mom and dad dance all around the living room. He knew how much they loved each other and he was glad to be their son. The song went off and another classic hit came right on behind it— "Planet Rock". Jack stepped back and started doing the robot, and mom Parker fell out laughing. Pooh Bear ran down the steps and joined right in with his father. Mom Parker loved when Jack spent time with his son, thinking to herself, "What would I do, if I ever lost one of these fools."

Deena was sitting at her computer streaming porn off the Internet. She was a member of the ten-inch-in-up-dick club. The only thing she liked more than a big dick was an even bigger one. But she really loved Rudy Ray and married him anyway, knowing that he wasn't packing. He treated her like a queen, that's all that mattered. Rudy Ray brought breakfast up and sat it on the bed. Him and Deena started eating and talking about what happened the night before.

"Rudy, you have to be careful, I don't know what I would do without you."

Rudy Ray started telling Deena how Jack was putting in work that night. The more he told her, the more her pussy got wet. Deena stood up and dropped her nightgown down on the floor, standing there naked with her nipples hard as ice. Rudy Ray grabbed her and put one of her breasts in his mouth. He loved to see his wife naked. She was tall with extremely long legs, and had one of the hairiest pussies he'd ever seen in his life.

Gutter Man was down Twenty-Sixth Street getting his hair cut at Busters Barbershop, when OG Son walked in the door. Gutter Man was pleased that he was on time for their meeting. OG Son was from Twenty-Eighth and Oakford. He ran everything from the Twenty-Fifth St. Bridge, clean over to Twenty-Six and Dickerson. And if a nigga was worth a fuck, he knew who they were. As the meeting began, everybody left the barbershop, even the barbers. Gutter Man started explaining his situation. OG Son needed him to take care of this problem. See, one of the four men that got killed that night was his nephew.

"Look Gutter Man, I need you to find out who this nigga is."

Gutter Man replied, "by already know who he is." OG Son leaned forward, as if to say, okay I'm listening.

"His name is BlackJack." OG Son's eyes got wide, and then he dropped his head.

Gutter Man said, "What, what, did I say something wrong? OG, is there a problem?"

OG Son raised his head, and looked dead into his eyes, then he spoke in a very serious tone. "Gutter Man, I need you to listen so you can hear me clearly. You have a real fucken problem on your hands, and you have undoubtedly barked up the wrong tree." OG Son knew all about BlackJack, they used to have some beef a few years back. OG Son sent twelve of his best men after Jack, one right after another, and not one of them ever came back. OG Son stood up and shook Gutter Man's hand, knowing that he was looking at a dead man. "Gutter Man, my dearest friend, my advice to you is to let this one go."

Gutter Man thought about it, but he had too much pride. Jack had put a gun to his head in front of the whole projects. Both men nodded and OG Son headed for the door. Gutter Man called out, "Yo OG, what about your nephew?"

OG Son said, "What about him? It looks like his mother and his father will have to get over it." He slammed the door behind him, and for the first time in Gutter Man's life, he felt like he had bitten off more than he could chew.

BlackJack was back to business on Mountain Drive. He was going to kill Gutter Man, anyway, so why not make some money off it. Jack sat there listening to Dave rant and rave on why he wanted Gutter Man dead so bad. "So, let me get this straight, you want him dead because he's fucking your wife."

Dave paused, then said, "You damn right, I'm supposed to be his right-hand man, and look at the thanks that I get. Do you know I followed that nigga one day? I was supposed to be collecting his money, but something just wasn't right, so I figured I would stop by my wife's job to bring her some lunch. As I was parking across the street from where she worked is when I saw her outside talking to Gutter Man. She hugged him, kissed him, then got in his car, and they pulled off. So, I followed them. He took her back to my house, the nerve of this mother fucker, so, I sat in the car, and waited about ten minutes, then I got ou, and went to the front window and peeked in. This nigga was running around in my living room, butt naked, dangling his balls, playing freeze tag with my wife, and all I kept hearing was, 'tag, you're it.'" BlackJack thought, "Man this nigga is fucking pathetic." Jack smiled and took his money, and the hit was on for both; Dave just didn't know it.

Rudy Ray and Deena laid in the bed chillin' after hours of having sex. She wished his dick was a lot bigger, but he made up for it in a lot of other ways. Feeling as though he handled his business, Rudy flicked on the television; there was a newsflash; it was about the shooting that took place last night in the projects. Rudy Ray grabbed the remote and turned it up. The news reporter said that the police did not have any suspects, and for anyone who has any tips to please call in. Rudy Ray picked up the phone to call Jack, but Jack and Tina were out at the market doing some shopping. They were all the way out in the suburbs, far far away from the troubles of the projects, so him and Tina could do some shopping in peace. Jack felt more comfortable there where he didn't have to watch his back. Mom Parker asked him what her limit was. Jack told her she didn't have one, just to shop til she dropped. And she did just that, they were in the checkout line, ready to get checked out, when Jack noticed there wasn't any milk in the cart. He told Tina to stay in line and that he would run and go get some. Halfway through the store, Jack's phone rang. It was Rudy Ray telling him about the newsflash, and that the police didn't have any suspects. In the middle of their conversation, all the power went out in the supermarket— the lights, cameras, and everything else that was electric. Jack was like, man what the fuck is going on here. Then Jack heard screaming coming from the front of the store, so he crept up there to see what the hell was going on. He had to duck down behind the display rack of real Mayo. He couldn't believe it, the market was getting stuck up, and these guys did their homework. It was three of them; one was manning the door; the other one was hitting the cash registers; and the third man went straight to the store manager's office where the safe was open. Jack kept calm as he reached down and pulled Norma from his hip. The one robbing the registers was standing over top of mom Parker, pointing his gun at the cashier. Mom Parker tried to move out of his way, but he grabbed her, and then banged her face against the counter. What the fuck was this nigga thinking? Jack peeked up and looked at both men, calculated the distance between the two, then he let off two shots—*block ah, block ah*—both men were dead before they hit the ground. The one that was in the manager's office heard the shots. He came out with the manager in one arm, and a gun to his head with the other. He saw both of his partners on the floor dead, so he began to panic, not even noticing Jack sneaking up behind him. Jack put his gun to the back of his head and clicked the hammer back. Then said, "Drop your weapon, and I wouldn't advise you to move." The robber reluctantly dropped his gun; the store manager ran to safety; then Jack pulled the trigger. The people in the store couldn't believe what they had just seen, but what was more important to them was this strange man just saved all of their lives.

Back at home, Pooh Bear was upstairs playing the game, when his mom and dad came in. He could hear his mom crying, so he went down the steps, saw the bruise on the side of his mom's face, and heard his dad telling her everything was going to be okay. Pooh Bear's heart sank into his stomach. He knew if someone had hurt his mom, they were already dead or getting ready to die. He knew his dad didn't play that shit when it came to his mother. He didn't want his dad to have to go away for murder. So, he got on his knees, and prayed that his dad would stop being so mad.

Gutter Man was sitting around the table discussing with his men the plan that needed to go into effect, immediately. BlackJack had to go, and it was no way around it. He told each man exactly what he had to do, and that they needed to secede by any means necessary.

Jack was really stressed out about the terrible events that had been happening. It had already been a long-ass day, and it still was early, so Jack decided that he needed his balls and his dick sucked. The first person that came to his mind was Cheryl, so he headed in her direction. When he spotted two men following him, Jack played it off like he didn't know what was going on. And he continued on his path until he got to Cheryl's house. He walked in the front door, and went right out the back, making his way back to Rudy Ray's house. Two minutes later, there was a knock at

Cheryl's door. She opened it, and said, "Can I help you?" There was a guy standing there asking if Jack was there. Rudy Ray came out of the kitchen with two beers in his hand, giving one to Jack. Jack was sitting at the dining room table, cleaning Norm and Norma. Rudy Ray sat at the other end of the table explaining to Jack why they needed to make a move. Jack already knew he had to kill Gutter Man. He just wanted the time to be right, but it had to be soon. Deena and mom Parker were on the phone. Deena was telling her about a shooting that took place at a supermarket out in the suburbs. Mom Parker was like "Why, what the hell is this world coming to," knowing damn well she was the reason they met their maker. Jack's phone started vibrating, so he pulled it off of his side to check it. It was a text message from Cheryl that said, "Hey, where did you go, bring that dick back around here?" with smiley faces all across the bottom. Jack started smiling; his mind went straight to the gutter; so, he told Rudy Ray that he would catch him later. BlackJack approached Cheryl's house. He could see that the door was slightly opened. "But Cheryl never keeps her door open," he was thinking. He pulled out Norm and Norma, and crept up to the door, and slowly pushed it open. Jack just stood there like his eyes were deceiving him; Cheryl and Lisa were dead. Lisa was lying face down, ass up, with two-bullet holes in the back of her head. Cheryl was sitting on the floor with her head slumped down between her chest. She took a bullet right to the face. You could still hear their mother upstairs calling down for one of her daughters to bring her something to eat. Jack reached over and closed Cheryl's eyes, then noticed that she had a note in her hand. He took the note and opened it, reading all of its content. Jack dropped the note and ran out of the house as fast as he could. The note said, "Your wife is next."

Jack called home to check on his wife and his son. Tina answered the phone and told Jack to please calm down. She could not understand what he was saying. Jack yelled, "Heebo!" Tina went silent, dropped the phone, then ran upstairs. See Heebo is a code word that Jack use to let his family know danger is on its way, and mom Parker needed to protect her and Pooh Bear. As she entered her room, she kicked off her flip flops to put on her sneakers, grabbed her gun and adjusted her bulletproof vest, then ran into Pooh Bear's room, shutting and locking the door. Pooh Bear jumped up out of his sleep, asking his mother what was going on. Mom Parker said, "Heebo, Pooh Bear, Heebo." Pooh bear knew exactly what to do—go to his secret spot and hide. Jack hung up after talking to Tina so he could call Dave. He told Dave that their plan had to be moved up, that Gutter Man had to die tonight. Dave agreed. So, the plan was now put into full motion. Rudy Ray was still chillin' and drinking beer while watching SportsCenter. Rudy Ray heard someone banging on his front door.

"Who the fuck is banging on my door like that?"

"Rudy it's me, Jack, open up!" Rudy hurried to the door and opened it. Jack came in and gave Rudy Ray the rundown, telling him that he was right, and they needed to move tonight. After getting everything ready to go, Jack and Rudy Ray sat in the car, locked and loaded, waiting on the signal from Dave. Gutter Man was cursing Dave the fuck out for coming to his house so late and uninvited.

"Look, Gutter Man, this couldn't wait until tomorrow, the money I collected for you today, it was ten grand short." Now he had Gutter Man's attention.

"What do you mean ten grand short?"

Dave was lying through his teeth, but he knew Gutter Man wouldn't live long enough to find out his treachery. As Dave was telling Gutter Man all these lies, Gutter Man's phone rang. He was so busy yelling; he didn't even bother to see who it was. "Hello." When he heard the voice, Gutter Man told Dave that he had to wait one second, that this call was very important. Gutter Man stepped to the side to continue his conversation. Now was the perfect time, so Dave sent his signal. It was a text that said, "Three, two, one." Gutter Man wasn't paying Dave any mind. He was just a laughing and joking on the phone, talking mad shit to Dave's wife. She was telling him how much bigger his dick was than Dave's, and that she was home alone and wanted to get fucked. "Oh really, well let me finish up this business with your husband, then I will send him on a dummy mission, and be right over." Then he hung up, cleared his throat, and said, "Now, Dave, where were we?" Jack got the signal that he was waiting for. Before him and Rudy Ray got out of the car, Jack popped both clips out of Norm and Norma, and just left one bullet in each chamber.

Rudy Ray said, "Man, what the fuck are you doing?"

Jack said, "Sorry Rudy, but this one is going to be up close, and personal."

Rudy Ray just shook his head, got out of the car and ran across the street to the dark side of Gutter Man's house. He could see them talking through the window. Rudy Ray took his riot pump and tapped on the window.

Gutter Ma said, "Dave, did you just hear something?"

Dave said, "No, I didn't hear anything."

As they continued talking, Rudy Ray tapped on the window again. Gutter Man stopped talking. "Dave, I know you just heard that, it's something over there by that fucking window."

Both men walked over and looked out the window, but didn't see anything. BlackJack kicked the front door open and both men spun around. All you heard was, *click,click,boom*. Rudy Ray blew Dave's whole back the fuck out. Gutter Man started pissing all over himself as he watched Jack point Norm and Norma right at him. Gutter Man started bitching and pleading his case. Jack wasn't trying to hear that shit, not one bit of it. So, Jack shot him in the stomach. The force from the bullet knocked him into the wall. As Gutter Man slid down the wall, begging for mercy, he left a trail of blood.

"Please stop, Jack."

"Did you just ask me to stop, you bitch-ass nigga? I got your mercy right here."

As Jack began to pistol whip his face, Gutter Man cried out, "Listen Jack, I got money, you can have it all."

Jack said, "No, you listen, and I want you to hear me very clearly." He put Norma to his ear, then pulled the trigger, blowing his brains all over the coffee table. Then Jack kneeled over the top of his body, spat in what was left of his face, then him and Rudy Ray burned his place down, just before they slipped off into the night.

CHAPTER 6

F ive years later, everything had been going good for Jack. It seemed
like Gutter Man was the only thing standing in his way, and since his
death, everything just fell right in line. BlackJack was a celebrity and he
knew it. Everybody respected him and showed him love; he felt like he
was in his old neighborhood. Jack was making all the money, and still
would break the dice game every now and then. He owned his own black-
poppy store and had five-water-ice stands all around the projects. The only
thing Jack didn't have a hand in was the drug game. It wasn't his thing. He
was a hustler and a killer, but not a drug dealer. Pooh Bear was now going
on seventeen; he had gotten tall, cut up, and all the young girls loved him.
Mom Parker looked like she was getting thicker with time. The Parker
family was doing great. Just before school started, BlackJack threw a huge
cookout for Pooh Bear on the last holiday in September. All his friends
were there—Ra Ra, Bay Boy, Joe Hot, and Leak. Joe Hot and Leak
became Pooh Bear's friends not long after that fight. Joe Hot figured, fuck
it, if you can't beat them, then join them. The music was playing, people
were laughing, and the children were dancing right in the middle of the
street. Rudy Ray was on the grill and Deena was making potato salad, and
right in the midst of all that, Will Smith's "Summertime" came on the
radio. Even the older people got up and started singing and dancing. "It's

43

summer, summer, summertime, it's summertime, let's just sit back and unwind. . .." The day couldn't have been better; the food was unlimited, and BlackJack paid for it all. His brother was up from North Carolina, and his half-sister was in from DC. BlackJack's brother's name was Otis, but everybody called him Holly Bop, or Bop, if you were considered family. Most people say he was twice as dangerous as Jack, but his terror was in the dirty South, not in Philadelphia. To anyone else, he looked like an everyday average Joe, but he was super smart, and just came home from doing a five-year bid. He had gotten thirty to sixty years in prison and was labeled a menace to society. He went into the law library by himself and gave all that time back. Fuck a lawyer, as far as he was concerned, he got him sent up the river, with no paddles. Jack's half-sister was pretty. She lived in Washington, D.C., by herself, and she had no kids. Her and Jack had the same dad, but different mothers; to Jack she was his full sister. As the cookout started winding down, mom Parker and Deena started cleaning up everything. While Jack, Rudy, Bop, and his sister played cards, Pooh Bear and all of his friends left to go out to the Wilson projects to another party; this was a house party, no adults, only teenagers. By the time Pooh Bear and his boys got to the party, it was packed. Everybody was there—all those Wilson hoes and all the want-to-be-Tasker gold diggers were in the house. As Pooh Bear, Ra Ra, Leak, and Joe Hot paid their dollars to get in, the DJ put on Fifty Cent's "Many Men," niggas started singing, "Many men, wish deaths upon me, blood in my eye dog I just can't see, they want to take my life away. . . ." Carmen saw Pooh Bear and his boys enter the party. She tapped her girlfriends—Sheema, Mya, and Chippy—letting them know Pooh Bear and his hommies were in the house. Now Carmen and her girlfriends were from Tasker but went anywhere there was a party. Carmen had a crush on Pooh Bear ever since she met him. She wanted to give him the pussy, but couldn't. She'd never been with a man before, but you couldn't tell. She had a gap that you could see from Philadelphia to New Jersey. She was tall with real long legs and was a cold-blooded tease. The rest of her team fucked anybody they thought had a few dollars. Even when they were little playing catch-a-girl-get-a-girl; when all the other girls were running for their lives, these bitches would slow down so that they would get caught. Carmen and her girls were making their way through the crowd and over to Pooh Bear and his boys, when a nigga named, Footty, stopped her.

"So, Carmen, when are you gonna let a nigga tap that." Then he smiled.

Carmen said, "In about one hundred years."

As she walked by, he yelled out, "I'll be dead in one hundred years."

She said, "I know, that means never." Carmen and her crew fell out laughing.

"I see you got jokes, right, you broke ass bitch." Carmen just flagged him because the party was poppin.'

BlackJack and his brother were shaking hands becaue he was about to hit the road and head back down South. Jack was disappointed that his brother had to leave so soon. But he understood, knowing that his brother was into new and positive things. He had a lot going on. He was in the middle of writing his own play, setting up his first awards banquet, and was in charge of the durms only American Idol contest that was sponsored by Fox 50. The ex-con was giving back to his community. Jack's sister said that she would stay for a couple more days, but she had to go home, also. Everybody was high off weed, except for Pooh Bear; he didn't smoke or drink, ever. It was not his twist, plus his dad told him to always be on point, and he was. After the slow song went off, the DJ put on Fat Joe's "Lean Back"—"Everybody do the rock away, lean back, lean back." As Pooh Bear leaned back, he bumped into E-money. E-money pushed him and said, "Yo, what the fuck you doin' hommie?" E-money was Footty's right-hand man. They ran the Wilson projects and called themselves the Buffalo Boys. It was Footty, E-money, Day Day, and Apple that made up their crew. They were into everything, like sticken niggas up, selling drugs, pills, and syrup; if it was illegal, they were bout' it bout' it. Footty was the worst of them, he stopped giving a fuck ever since his father got killed five years ago. Pooh Bear turned around and had some words with E-money. Carmen tapped her girls and said, "Here comes the bullshit y'all, let's go." She reminded Pooh Bear that they were not in their neighborhood. Pooh Bear peeped the move and then walked away, signaling his crew to roll out. Pooh Bear and his boys left the party. As they passed by Yo-Yo's Bar, Footty and his crew, with six other boys, ran up on them. They turned facing the ten boys. Ra Ra said, "Look Footty, we don't want any trouble." E-money said, "It is too late for that," then punched Ra Ra in his face. The shit was on. Joe Hot sucker punched Day Day, and Leak was all over Apple. Pooh Bear and Footty locked asses. Everybody came out of the bar to watch the free-for-all in the middle of the street. Pooh Bear and Footty were getting it the fuck in. For the first time in Pooh Bear's life, he had a fight on his hands. They went blow for blow, and Footty was just as fast as he was. He hit Footty with a one, two. Footty ducked, then came back with two body shots. Footty hit Pooh Bear with two-straight jabs, and Pooh Bear hit him with an uppercut followed by a right cross. Pooh Bear had his hands full. So, it was nothing that he could do about what was happening to Ra Ra. Ra Ra was a tall, light-skinned-Playboy-ass nigga who was light in his ass. His body couldn't withstand the punishment them Wilson niggas were dishing out. It was four niggas on his ass, and eventually he went down, but the nigga still didn't stop. They started stomping him with Tims and kicking him in his face. And Joe Hot couldn't see out of neither one of his eyes. Luckily the bar owner called the police, and when they arrived, the ten boys took off running. The police didn't bother even giving chase; they knew if them cats hit the projects, they would be impossible to find. All four boys were rushed to University Hospital. The police contacted the boys' parents and told them what happened. In less than an hour, BlackJack and mom Parker came into the emergency room. The doctor asked them if they were the parents of all the boys. They said, "No, just the parents of Kobe Parker, but how are the other boys doing?" The doctor said, "They are not doing so well. Leak and Kobe can go home, but the other three will be admitted." On the way home, BlackJack could see something was really bothering his son, but all three of them road home in silence. Jack pulled up in front of the door and left the car running. Mom Parker knew BlackJack wanted to talked to his son, so she got out of the car, and went in the house without anybody telling her to. Then Pooh Bear got out, and got in the front passenger seat. He started to explain what happened, and Jack cut him off.

"But dad—"

He tried to explain again, and Jack cut him off again, and said, "All I want to know, is what you are going to do about it?"

Pooh Bear lifted his head up and looked his dad in the face, and said, "I want to kill that mother fucker."

Before Jack knew it, he'd slapped the shit out of Pooh Bear and told him to watch his fucken mouth in his presence. Jack realized what he had just done. He knew his son meant no disrespect; he was just upset. So, BlackJack apologized and asked him if he really meant what he just said. Pooh Bear said, "yes," then Jack pulled off. Mom Parker called Deena telling her Pooh Bear was okay. BlackJack's sister was trying to get her attention in the background, but mom Parker paid her no mind. She was so distraught about what was going on, all she could do was cry.

Jack pulled up to his storage garage where he kept all his extra food and merchandise for his store. Him and Pooh Bear got out; Jack unlocked all the locks, and they went in. Jack took Pooh Bear with him all the way to the back, and removed some fake cabinets off of the wall. He pulled out a small chest and sat it on the floor. Pooh Bear said, "Dad, what is that?" Jack opened up the chest and Pooh Bear's eyes lit up. It was five-brand-new-40-caliber weapons; BlackJack picked up one of the guns and gave it to Pooh Bear.

Pooh Bear said, "What is this for?"

"Well, you said you want to kill Footty, right?"

Pooh Bear said, "Yes."

"Okay then, the next time you see him, you walk right up to him, and blow his mother fucken brains out?" Jack then closed the chest to put it back. Pooh Bear saw a smaller chest in there, and asked what that one was for. BlackJack said, "That is for you."

Pooh Bear said, "If it is for me, then let me see."

Jack reached up, grabbed the box, and opened it. There were two objects covered in a gold-colored cloth. Jack told him to take a look. Pooh Bear removed the cloth, and saw two more brand-new-40-caliber weapons, except these were a whole lot different. They were custom-made with extended clips. Pooh Bear picked them up. They felt like they were tailor-made for his hands. He raised them up to the light, to get a better look; as his eyes hit the handles of the guns, he saw an inscription written on each one; one said Mac; the other said Mindy. Pooh Bear said, "Dad why can't I take these, if they are mine?"

Jack said, "When you're ready, I mean really ready, they will be here for you."

Jack put everything back, and him and Pooh Bear left. Ra Ra was feeling a lot better, and even though all six of his babies' mamas were at the hospital, not one of them had anything bad to say. They were just happy that he still was alive. Ra Ra had got the worst of the ass woopin's that they all took. He had a broken rib and his face took a beating. Pooh Bear, Joe Hot, and Leak went to see Ra Ra. As they walked in, Ra Ra smiled, and said, "What's up my niggas?" Ra Ra told his babies' mothers to take the kids over to Children's Hospital, to McDonald's, so he and his boys could talk. After the girls left, Ra Ra stopped smiling, and had a serious look on his face. He told his crew, "I don't know about y'all, but I ain't doing no more fucking fighting, I am about to turn it up on these niggas." Leak and Joe Hot looked puzzled, but Pooh Bear knew exactly where he was coming from. Pooh Bear began telling them about his plan, and that he wanted to kill Footty. He also told them that he had a present for each one of them the next time that they were altogether. They all shook hands, and Pooh Bear, Leak, and Joe Hot rolled out.

About ten thirty that night, Carmen called Pooh Bear on the phone. He wasn't going to answer because he didn't recognize the number, but he answered it anyway, thinking that it might be Ra Ra. "Hello."

"What's up, baby?"

"Who this?"

"It's Carmen."

"Yo' what's up, Carmen? How did you get my number?"

"I got it from Joe Hot. I told him to tell you the next time he saw you that I wanted to give you some pussy, so he told me to tell you myself, and gave me your number. Well?"

"Well, what?"

"Do you want the pussy or not?"

Pooh Bear wasn't about to turn down no sex. "Of course, I want it."

"Well, my mom won't be home until tomorrow morning, and my brother's down in Atlantic City."

Pooh Bear said, "Okay, I'll be right over."

Two minutes later, Pooh Bear was knocking on Carmen's door. She answered the door in a see-through nightgown and nothing underneath. Pooh Bear went inside and sat down on the sofa. Carmen asked him if he wanted something to drink, then went into the kitchen and got it for him. As she was bringing him his drink, Pooh Bear could see the gap between her legs, and his dick started getting hard. She put the drink down in front of him and went and put a slow jam CD in the CD player. When she bent over, all Pooh Bear could see was ass and pussy. Carmen walked back over and straddled Pooh Bear, kissing him; she could feel his dick getting harder in his pants and wondered if she was really ready to have sex. Pooh Bear told her to get up and go lay down on the couch, and she did. As she got up, Pooh Bear was like what the fuck? The front of his pants was soaking wet from her juices. Pooh Bear took off all his clothes. She took one look at his dick and closed her eyes. Pooh Bear got on top of her. He could tell from how nervous she was acting that it had to be her first time. He opened up her legs and told her to relax. As he slipped the head of his dick into her pussy, she screamed, pushed him off of her, and ran into the kitchen. Pooh Bear jumped up, dick just a swinging, and went to her and said he was sorry and that he was going to get dressed and leave. Carmen grabbed him and said, "No, don't leave, I want you to have my virginity,

49

it just hurt a little, that's all. Can we please try it again?" She grabbed Pooh Bear and started kissing him; tongue all down his throat. She had Pooh Bear on fire. He just lifted her up onto the deep-freezer, and then slid in between her legs. He asked her if she was ready, she said "yes," and pop went the weasel; she was a virgin no more. As Pooh Bear slid more and more of his dick into her, she just grabbed him, and dug her nails deep into his back, until he washed all of her worries away, with a pussy full of come.

CHAPTER 7

M om Parker and Pooh Bear were talking. She was telling him it was better for him to go to Audenreid High School than Southern because it was closer to home, and that his daddy went to the school back in the day. Audenreid is a good school now, but it wasn't back when Jack went. When he went there it was called the prison on the hill, literally. It was a school on a hill that took two flights of steps to get to the front door. And to add insult to the community, it had bars all over the windows. The school was dirty, and the only thing it had going for it, was its famous marble hall. If you were not from around Tasker, every day after school, the twenty-nine-bus-trolley line would get pulled off the wires, and you would get your ass kicked right then and there. Pooh Bear didn't really want to go to Southern, but he knew all the niggas from Wilson went there, and he didn't want to seem like he was scared or running by choosing another school. But he knew his mom was right, so he chose Audenreid. BlackJack and Pooh Bear were at the neighborhood Game Stop picking up the new Madden. Pooh Bear was the toughest young boy in South Philadelphia, I mean he wasn't a legend like Black Gene or 40 Ounce, but he was up-and-coming; he bet large amounts of money on himself, often winning the majority of his games. He hung out down Twenty-Second and Manton Street, over a brother named Big Buddha's house, where he played poker and Madden all day. Big Buddha was cool as shit, that's where all the young hustlers would hang out, playing cards and talking shit after eating from Hyons. Pooh Bear called Big Buddha up, told him that he had the new Madden, and the shit was on. As Pooh Bear walked out of Game Stop, his whole expression changed. And BlackJack could see it. Footty was standing right in front of him, talking on the payphone, with his back turned, slippin' like a motherfucker. Pooh Bear went to reach, then thought about it. Was he really ready to kill somebody? BlackJack peeped the whole situation, and never said a word, but said to himself, "My son got a lot of heart, but not the heart of a killer." Then they got in the car and left.

Two weeks later, Pooh Bear was sitting in his recliner chair sleep with his controller in his lap. The TV was still playing when his phone rang. It was Carmen. "What's up, baby girl?"

"What's up, big daddy, won't you come over here and tighten a sister up?"

Pooh Bear said, "Okay, I will be there in a minute," then hung the phone up. He went to get up, then fell down, and went back to sleep. Twenty minutes later, Pooh Bear's phone rang again.

"Hello, did you fall back to sleep, are you coming or what?"

"Okay okay Carmen, I will be right there." Pooh Bear hung the phone up, and for some mysterious reason, he fell back to sleep. He was tired as shit from kicking niggas' asses on Madden for two days straight. Thirty minutes later, Pooh Bear felt like something was dancing on his face. He opened his eyes wide, but his brain did not register what he was seeing. So he closed his eyes again and then it registered. The whole kitchen was on fire. Pooh Bear jumped up, ran into the kitchen, and tried to put the fire out, but it was too much. He ran back through the living room as the fire started shooting out of the walls. It was an electrical fire that had been burning for quite some time. Pooh Bear couldn't breathe, but he knew his mother and father were upstairs in the bed sleep. He ran up the steps and kicked his mom and dad's door open. Jack jumped up with his guns drawn, ready to shoot, until he saw it was Pooh Bear.

"What the hell is wrong with you?"

Pooh Bear said, "Dad, we got to get out of this house, it is on fire!"

Jack jumped up, pushing on mom Parker to get up. "Tina, the house is on fire, you have to wake up!"

After waking up, all three of them ran down the steps and out the front door. Pooh Bear fell to the ground, gasping for air. Mom Parker and Blackjack went next door to the neighbor's house. BackJack put Norm and Norma in the closet and went back outside to wait for the fire department. The house was burning bad. Rudy Ray and Deena ran up and only saw BlackJack and Pooh Bear, so they asked where was Tina. Before Jack could answer, somebody in the crowd said she must be still in the fire. After hearing that, Pooh Bear thought his mom was still in there, so he jumped up, and ran back into the burning house. Jack tried to grab him, but he was too fast. The fire was out of control. The house was burning to the ground, and Pooh Bear was still in there. Jack wanted his boy, and tried to get back into the house to get him, but the people wouldn't let him. Then there was a big explosion and the house started caving in. As firefighters arrived, they asked if anybody was still in the house. Jack fell to his knees, and Deena said "yes," then the whole house collapsed.

After the sad sad funeral, I will say that again, after the sad sad funeral, Footty couldn't believe that in just five years, he'd lost his mother and father. Even though his mother was on dope, and he'd sold it to her at one time or another, he still loved her. Now it was only him left. First, his dad, Gutter Man, and now, his mom was dead. He was the only child, and his grandparents died before he was born. He swore that he would kill the man responsible for his father's death. He just needed to find out who he was.

BlackJack, mom Parker, and Pooh Bear were having dinner at the Red Cross. Pooh Bear realized that his mother was not in the house. The fire was getting stronger by the second. It was too dangerous for him to go back from which he came, so he jumped out the back bathroom window and got out safely. Dinner was over and mom Parker was cleaning up when a Red Cross aid told her that the Tasker Tenant Council had just called and told them that they had a house for her, and it was ready for them to move right in. The address was 1805 E. Mifflin Street, smack dead in the center of the Tasker projects. Rudy Ray was coming back from across the tracks. He had just left Twenty-Second and Christian Street, a few blocks from where he spent his childhood. He was standing on Twenty-Third and Washington Avenue, when he noticed the same SUV come by for the third time; once on Twenty-First St., and again on Twenty-Second; now here it was again on Twenty-Third. His instincts kicked right in. He jogged across the street to a hot dog stand and bought two hot dogs and a soda. He tried to obstruct the SUV's line of sight, but the SUV parked right on the corner where the hot dog cart was. Rudy Ray looked out the corner of his eye, but he couldn't see who was in the Yukon because the windows were tented. He paid for his food, then walked off in the opposite direction. The guys in the SUV said to one another, "I think he's on to us." They both then locked and loaded their weapons and said it doesn't even matter. As one of them got out of the SUV, Rudy Ray made a left onto the Twenty-Fifth St. bridge thinking that he might be able to use the large concrete legs, holding up the bridge, for cover. As Rudy Ray looked back, he saw a man he didn't recognize closing in on him. Rudy Ray took off, cutting back and forth between the traffic and the bridge, but it wasn't helping. The shooter was in hot pursuit, and Rudy Ray was getting tired. Then out of nowhere, the SUV tried to hit him. Rudy Ray fell but got back up and started running. He made a left down Dickerson Street and a quick right up Taylor, but that was a bad decision. The block was too long, and Rudy Ray was out of breath. He tried to run into some people's houses, but they were SHUTTING, and locking their doors. Halfway up the block, Rudy Ray could see the SUV turn and wait on the corner. He turned and looked in the other direction. The killer was coming towards him. Rudy Ray ran up the steps and began banging on every door, begging for anyone to please let him in. But no one would. Rudy Ray went to jump off the steps, when the killer fired two shots, *block ah, block ah.* One of the bullets hit Rudy Ray in his leg, in midair, snapping the bone clean in half. Rudy Ray let out a loud scream, and then he hit the ground. All you could hear were police sirens coming from a mile away. Rudy Ray tried to get back up, but the killer shot him again, *block ah, block ah.* Rudy Ray's life started flashing before his eyes, then the killer stood over top of him, and gave him two more, *block ah, block ah,* then everything went black.

Ra Ra was becoming more and more unstable. Since that ass whippin' that he took at Yo-Yo's Bar, it seemed like every time that he got into an argument with somebody, he was either pulling his gun, or flashing his knife on them. Deep depression was starting to set in, and nobody could tell how bad it was, not even him. Pooh Bear pulled up, showing Ra Ra his new whip that BlackJack had just bought him. It was a Nissan Pulsar— a nice little sports car with a stick shift. Ra Ra hopped in, and the boys went joyriding. Meanwhile, Carmen, Sheema, Mya, and Chippy were at Carmen's house chillen,' they were smoking weed, drinking, and doing just what girls were famous for— talking shit about other people. When Carmen started telling her girls how her and Pooh Bear were fucking, none of them believed her because they knew she was a virgin. Carmen said, "For real y'all, I wouldn't lie, that nigga be tearing this pussy up." The girls laughed, but Chippy was a little jealous because she wanted to fuck Pooh Bear; Mya was jealous too, because she always wanted to fuck Carmen. She knew Carmen was a virgin, and that pussy was pure, and those juices would be nice and sweet. Then Sheema butted in, with her nipples hard and her mouthwatering.

"How about we call Pooh Bear and his boys up, and we have an orgy?"

"Girl shut up you freak." Carmen replied.

"No for real, I'm serious." The girls looked at each other and said fuck it, let's do it.

Pooh Bear's phone started ringing. He checked it and saw it was Carmen, so he let it go to his voicemail. She hung up and called him right back; he let his voicemail pick up again. He wasn't dissing Carmen, it's just that him and Ra Ra were getting their balls licked from two young freaks they'd just met while out joyriding. I mean these bitches was just flat-out whores. An hour ago, they were licking on water ice, now they were licking on some dick. Pooh Bear and Ra Ra didn't care, they were never going to see those bitches again, anyway. They were down on Seventeenth and Burks. It wasn't their neck of the woods. As Pooh Bear and Ra Ra got finished taking these sluts for bad, it was time to go. The girls got mad. "Oh, so you are going to just bust all up in our faces, and just leave. Y'all niggas from South Philly ain't shit." Pooh Bear and Ra Ra were cracking the fuck up. As they were walking out the front door, one of the girls looked out the window, and said, "Fuck both of y'all," in an angry tone. Her brother was standing across the street and asked her if everything was okay. Pooh Bear and Ra Ra just stood there and looked because they did not know who the fuck he was talking to. Pooh Bear went to get the car. As he pulled up, Ra Ra went to get in, but the boy across the street asked him what the fuck was he looking at. Without saying a word, Ra Ra pulled his gun and started clappin' at this nigga—*bloom bloom, bloom, bloom bloom, bloom, bloom*—The boy started giving it back—*bang bang, bang bang, bang bang bang bang bang, bang bang*—Pooh Bear rolled down his window and started shooting too—*block ah, block ah, block ah, block block,block* ah—then niggas started coming out of the woodworks. Pooh Bear told Ra Ra to get the fuck in the car so they could go. Ra Ra got in just in time, as a nigga was walking right up on them with a chopper. Pooh Bear hit the gas, then the nigga hit the trigger. And all you could see were sparks. I mean he tore the whole fucken street up and didn't hit a mother fucken thing. After Pooh Bear got far enough away, he asked Ra Ra what the fuck was he thinking. Ra Ra turned and just stared at Pooh Bear. Pooh Bear looked right into his eyes and could tell that his soul was gone.

Deena called BlackJack and Tina crying, and very hysterical, saying she just got a call that Rudy Ray had been killed on Twenty-Fourth and Taylor Street. She asked if they could meet her at the University Hospital. Within minutes Jack and mom Parker were running through the emergency room doors. Deena was down on her knees in front of the doctor, begging and pleading for him to tell her that it wasn't so. The doctor said, "Ma'am, your husband did, in fact, pass away," Jack lowerd his head, "but the paramedics were able to bring him back. He is in a coma, right now, in very critical condition. He was shot five times, and his left leg was shattered, only time and a lot of prayer will save him." After his surgery was over, Deena sat next to Rudy Ray's hospital bed, holding his hand, and talking to him. Tears rolled down her face as she looked at all those tubes in his body. Knowing that he was in a coma and may never wake up, she started reminiscing about when her and Rudy Ray first met. It was the spring of '96, and they both were at Elmwood skating rink in Southwest Philly, at Seventy-First and Elmwood St. Rudy Ray kept trying to holler at her, but she wouldn't give him the time of day. But Rudy Ray wasn't going to stop until he at least had her name or her number. Elmwood skating rink was the spot. It seemed like all the girls that were fast and hot in the ass knew how to skate. Rudy Ray couldn't keep his eyes off of Deena. Every time she would look his way, he would try to show off. Rudy Ray was a good skater, but Deena was better. The DJ put on LL Cool J's "Around the Way Girl," and the skating rink went wild. They were skating forward, backwards, on one leg, doing splits, running train lines, just having a ball. Then Deena fell and Rudy stopped to help her. And by the end of the night, Rudy Ray had her name and her number. The rest was history. "Miss, Miss . . ." The nurse snapped Deena out of her daze. "Is everything okay?"

Deena said, "Yes."

The nurse said, "Will you be staying with us tonight?"

Deena said, "I'll be staying until he wakes up."

CHAPTER 8

B lackJack knew Twenty-Fourth and Taylor Street well. It was the block that he caught his first two bodies on when he was just fifteen years old, and the people on the block loved him for it. Ever since that day he saved those two little girls from being abducted. Jack stopped at a couple of well-known houses on the block where he could get some information from. None of the information he was getting was any good, until he stopped in the speakeasy on the corner. The speakeasy was owned by a nigga named Duck. Duck was a laid-back hustler, but he always had his ear to the streets. He told Jack that there had been a hit put out for him and Rudy Ray, and the nigga pulling the strings carried a lot of weight. Duck didn't know what his name was, but he did know the names of the two hit men. He told Jack one of the nigga's names was jaBrill from Seventh Street, and the other one was named Kato from the Passyunk projects. BlackJack gave Duck a couple thousand dollars and a handshake, telling him that he would see him at another time. Pooh Bear checked his cell phone. He had two missed messages from Carmen. Both messages said, "This is Carmen, it's very important, please call me back as soon as possible." Pooh Bear called, then she told him what her and her girls wanted to do. Pooh Bear called his boys up, and the party was on. Pooh Bear and Ra Ra pulled up just as Leak and Joe Hot were about to knock on Carmen's door. Leak and Joe Hot walked over to the car asking Pooh Bear who car they just stole. Pooh Bear got out with his keys waving in the air. It's mine, home boy. As the boys were talking, Chippy was peeking out of the window, telling the other girls hear they come. Pooh Bear rang the doorbell, and nobody answered. So, he rang it again, and nobody answered, again.

Joe Hot said, "Man, these bitches are playing games, we the fuck out."

Just as they were about to leave, they heard Sheema say, "Who is it?"

"It's us, baby girl."

Then Sheema opened the door, and all you seen was her standing their ass naked. "Are yall coming in or what?" The boys hurried up inside. She closed the door then turned on the lights, Carmen, Mya, Chippy, and Sheema were all naked with baby oil all over their bodies. Carmen was tall, with long legs, a gap, and a nice little camel toe. Mya was gorgeous and petite, with her nipples pierced. Chippy had a fat ass with a nice little bush between her legs. Sheema had the fattest pussy out of all of them.

"Well, what y'all niggas waiting for, come up out of those clothes," the girls replied.

"And whoever got the biggest dick, that's who I want to fuck first," said Sheema.

The boys didn't waste any time getting naked, and the girls weren't disappointed neither. Joe Hot got down on his knees and started licking all over Chippy's ass; he opened those ass cheeks and put his tongue all up in it; Chippy started standing on her tippy toes, shaking like a mother fucker.

Carmen said, "Sorry boys, ain't nobody getting this pussy but Pooh Bear."

So, Ra Ra grabbed Sheema by her hair, moved her over to the couch, and pushed her to her knees. She said, "Stop being so rough." Ra Ra told her to shut the fuck up, as he smashed her head into the corner of the chair, then took the pussy from behind. Leak had Mya sitting on top of the armchair eating her pussy like no tomorrow. His face was all wet and he had cream all over his chin. Pooh Bear was fingering Carmen; he was sucking all over her titties as she was stroking his dick; he was making her come with his fingers. Ra Ra was fucken Sheema so hard, she had tears rolling down her face, but she never told him to stop.

"Who your fucken daddy, bitch?"

"You are, Ra Ra, but it hurt so bad."

"Shut the fuck up and take this dick you whore." Ra Ra was tripping, but Sheema was loving it.

Joe Hot had Chippy sitting on his lap, with her legs in the air, and his dick in her ass. His dick was stretching her ass twice the size that it was. Leak switched places with Mya. She was sucking the shit out of his dick, as he rubbed the side of her face, telling her how good it was feeling. Pooh Bear laid Carmen down on the floor and put her legs up on his shoulders. She was so tight, he had to force his dick in; that shit almost made him come. Carmen couldn't take it, but she was in love with Pooh Bear, so she took the pain. Pooh Bear was being gentle with her, but he needed to get his whole dick in her pussy. Leak picked Mya's little ass up and sat her on top of his dick. As he was walking around the living room fucking her, all you could smell in the air was sex. Joe Hot pulled his dick right out of Chippy's ass and put it right back in her pussy, never even wiping it off. But she didn't care that shit was feeling too good. Ra Ra made Sheema get up and lay across the arm of the couch, as he continued to pound her pussy. Leak was holding Mya up in midair, popping the shit out of her. He told her that he was about to come.

She said, "I'm not on the pill, so don't come in me."

Leak said, "I can't hold back any longer."

So, he pulled out and shot come all through the air. The shit was everywhere. Carmen told Pooh Bear that she loved him, she wanted to be his girl, and that she wouldn't give the pussy to nobody else, but him. He told her to please stop talking. For the first time in his life, he wanted to eat some pussy. He slid down between her legs and put her clit in his mouth and began to suck and nibble on it. Carmen didn't know what was happening. She was losing control of her body. Pooh Bear was tasting pussy juice for the first time, and it wasn't bad, at all. Joe Hot knew he was putting his thing down because Chippy was moaning and loving every minute of it. Joe Hot stroked his dick until he couldn't take it anymore. He pulled out shooting it all over her stomach and her titties; some of it even reached up to her neck. Ra Ra was still pounding away. Sheema was getting a little sore from Ra Ra being so rough. She could tell he was about to come because the strokes got a lot shorter and faster. Sheema tried to get up, but Ra Ra wouldn't let her. Then he pinned her down and exploded inside of her pussy.

She said, "No Ra Ra, I'm not on any birth control." But he didn't care, he still was letting it go all up in her, until his dick was empty. "Why did you just do that, Ra Ra?"

"Because you wanted me to."

"I know, but I might get pregnant."

"So, what, don't you want to have a baby?"

"Well, yes, but not now, I'm only 18."

Pooh Bear was really liking the taste of Carmen's pussy. He started licking harder and faster. Carmen's body started to go into convolutions. Pooh Bear licked faster. She started twitching, and turning, and moaning, pushing down on Pooh Bear's head. She felt her body lock up, and her pussy started to tingle. She banged her fist on the floor, then that was all she wrote. Come started shooting out of her pussy like a sprinkler. Pooh Bear jumped up and didn't know what was going on. Carmen was a squirter, and he didn't even know it. Carmen couldn't stop it from shooting out, she didn't know what was going on, all she knew was that it felt incredible. Pooh Bear stood there and watched it shoot all over the rug. At first, he was confused, but now, he was turned on. He stroked his dick until he came, then he stood over top of her, cumming all over her body, and she just laid there and let him.

Footty and his boys were down on South Street. They stopped at Fourth and South to get some pizza. This place had the best pizza in Philadelphia, and bad bitches were all over the place. E-money was in a bad mood, like he always is. These niggas were strapped, and cops were all over the place. Neither one of them gave a fuck. As far as they were concerned, the cops could get it too. You could tell that they were out on some bullshit because four girls walked past them, one of them had a booty that was just plain stupid, and Footty and his crew tried to talk to them. The girls ignored them and kept walking. Apple said, "Yall bitches dirty anyway." They stopped in the gap. The security guard was all over them. He walked up on Footty asking him did he need any help. Footty said, "Yes, I need some help, come here." The guard walked over to him. Footty pulled up his shirt and told the guard to mind his mother fucken business, or else. The guard looked around and went and stood back at the door. They wanted to rob the place, but it was just too many people. So they took pretty much whatever they wanted, then left. E-money saw his old girlfriend standing on the next corner, her, and her boyfriend. E-money got even madder.

"Look at this stink ass bitch right here, Footty."

"Who?"

"Tammy."

"Where?"

"Right there, standing on the corner, with that lame ass nigga."

"Damn, she trying to play you, dog. You better go and handle that." Footty was piping E-money the fuck up because him and Tammy had been broken up for over three years.

E-money walked up to Tammy and her boyfriend. "Oh so you trying to play me, right? Tammy was looking dumb founded, she turned to look behind her, then back at E-money. "Yes, you bitch, I'm talking to you and that joe-sausage-head-ass nigga right there." Tammy didn't know what to say, so she didn't say anything. E-money punched her in her mouth and pulled his burner out and shot the boy twice in his chest. Then they just walked off, going about their business, as nothing ever happened. BlackJack got a call from Duck telling him he had some more information. He told him jaBrill and Kato both were very dangerous, but jaBrill would be the easier one to find, because he was addicted to pancakes and syrup, and often hung out at this deli on Seventh and Snyder. Jack was also advised to be careful because jaBrill didn't look like who he really was. He was a short-brown-skinned brother and wore glasses that made him look like a nerd. But he was a stone-cold killer. Kato would be the harder of the two. He stayed in the Passyunk projects and only moved when it was necessary. If not, he stayed put. There were only two ways out of those projects, the front entrance, and the one by the Schoolkill Expressway. Jack thanked him and then hung up. He knew his plans had to be flawless, but flawless or not, both jaBrill and Kato were going to die for what they did to Rudy Ray. Back at the hospital, mom Parker was at the information desk so she could go up and visit Rudy Ray and Deena. She got her pass and got on the elevator. She got off on the eighth floor and made a left. She could see Deena standing outside of Rudy Ray's room talking to the doctor. The closer she got, the more she heard. Deena was asking the doctor if he had lost his mind. The doctor said, "It would be for the best," and then he walked off. Deena started crying. Mom Parker hugged her asked what was wrong. "Tina, they want me to pull the plug on Rudy, what is wrong with them, are they crazy? I would never do anything like that." As she continued to cry in mom Parker's arms, Tina told her not to worry, that everything was going to be okay. Rudy will pull through all of this. As soon as she said that all the alarms went off in Rudy Ray's room. The doctors and nurses came running. Rudy Ray had flatlined and all his vital signs on the monitor were reading zero. Deena snapped the fuck out. "O my God, no!" Mom Parker was holding her back, "No God, please don't take him." The nurses performed CPR on Rudy, while the doctors were getting the electric defibrillator ready. The doctors told the nurses to give him thirty ccs of medicine. Then Deena screamed out. The doctors and nurses were working frantically. Deena fell to her knees. It seemed like the doctors and the nurses were moving in slow motion. They were pointing, and pumping, and putting oxygen into Rudy Ray's body, then all you heard was "Clear!" They hit Rudy Ray with both defibrillators. His body jumped up off the hospital bed. The doctor said "Clear!" then hit him again. Tina and Deena were holding each other, crying. Rudy Ray's body jumped off the bed again. The monitor was still reading zero. The doctor dropped his head, took off his gloves, and looked at Deena shaking his head. He looked at his watch and told the nurse the time of death. Then he heard a beep, and then another one. The nurse said, "Doctor, I think we have a pulse." The numbers on the monitor started going up. The doctors had saved Rudy Ray's life again, and Deena couldn't believe that God had answered her prayers. Rudy Ray was still breathing and alive.

A month and some change later, Sheema was in the bathroom taking a pregnancy test. It had been two weeks since the last time she'd seen her last period, plus she was always feeling sick in the morning. She couldn't believe it. Ra Ra had gotten her pregnant. It must have happened that day they had that orgy at Carmen's house. She took another one just to be sure and that one came up with a plus sign too. "Oh, God, what am I going to do?" She picked the phone up and called Ra Ra, but Pooh Bear, Joe Hot, Leak, and Ra Ra, were out riding on their four-wheelers. They were all hungry, so they decided to ride up to Forty-Ninth and Woodland Avenue to get some Jamaican food. They hit Graysferry Avenue, then the southwest bridge. Joe Hot was laughing and holding up traffic while doing a willie all the way across the bridge. Ra Ra's phone was ringing. It was Sheema. Ra Ra answered her call but couldn't hear what she was saying because the four-wheelers were too loud. So, he told her he would call her back. The boys hit the Jamaican spot and got their grub on. Then they road to Twenty-Fifth and Snyder's playground where the basketball games were being played. They were being played right across the street from the Wilson projects. Sitting in the crowd was Footty, E-money, Day Day, and Apple. "Look at these dumb-ass niggas right here," Footty said. Pooh Bear and his crew pulled up and stopped to watch the game. Tasker was playing Wilson, and Wilson was losing. Pooh Bear spotted Footty and his boys in the crowd. "Now isn't the time," Pooh Bear thought, right here across the street from the police station. He didn't think so, so he told his crew they were out. They started their four-wheelers and began to leave when Footty started shooting at them—*bang, bang, bang bang bang, bang bang*—but the four-wheelers were so loud, they didn't even know they were being shot at, until Leak got grazed across his arm. Pooh Bear and his crew did half doughnuts, spinning back around and returned fire. People were running, ducking, and diving out of the way of the bullets, the shit was crazy.

BlackJack had been scoping jaBrill out for the last thirty days. He knew when and where he would be, and he knew what time he would be hanging out at the deli. Jack had already paid somebody to play along with his plan. All he needed the guy to do was play his part, and jaBrill's ass would be grass. Jack watched as jaBrill walked into the deli. He had two of his hommies that he would meet there and talk business. Jack walked in and sat at the table. He told the guy that he had paid that it was now time to play along. Jack said, "So what do you mean you don't have the money?" When jaBrill heard the word money, he started ear hustling. So Jack repeated it a little louder, making sure jaBrill would hear. "What do you mean you don't have the money, you made me bring you all these pancakes and syrup and you don't have the money? Don't you know this shit is the best in town? This should cost forty-five dollars an ounce." jaBrill was like, "What do this nigga got, it must be that blueberry tusk. I should jam his ass right now." The man was playing his part. jaBrill was eating that bullshit right up. Jack took the bookbag he had and pulled out a gallon of blueberry tusk. "Man, you can't find this shit nowhere." Jack put the tusk back into the bookbag and zipped it closed. "Well, I will tell you what, I will bring it back down here tomorrow, is that when you will have the money?" The man said "Yes," then him and Jack agreed to meet the next day at four thirty. jaBrill's mouth was watering. He could taste that blueberry tusk already, he just needed to get it. Jack got up to leave, but jaBrill stopped him by calling him a different name.

"Yo, whats up, Sammy?" Jack turned and looked. jaBrill walked over and shook his hand. "What's up hommie, when did you get out? Your name is Sammy, right?"

Jack said, "No, my name is B J."

"Oh, damn, that's right, my bad, what's up anyway, my nigga?"

"Do I know you from somewhere?"

"All, come on dog, you don't remember me? We were locked up together." Jack didn't know this nigga from a can of fucken paint, but his plan was working. Jack took a good look at him, then laughed it off.

"Yes, yes, what's up man, how have you been?"

"I've been good, what brings you down this way?"

"Nothing really, I was just passing through."

"I thought I would never see you again after you got out."

"Your name is jaBrill, right?"

jaBrill thought he had a real live one. "Yes, it's me in the flesh, what are you doing right now?"

Jack knew this was his cue. "Nothing, why what's up?"

"Well, I'm about to go over to my people's house, and fall back. We're having a little get together, you should come."

Jack said, "This shit can't be this easy."

jaBrill said, "Do they come any dumber than this nigga? No!"

"I don't have anything to do, lead the way."

Both men walked and talked until they reached Seventh and Wolf. jaBrill was going to kill this nigga and take what he had in his bag, but Jack had other plans. jaBrill took Jack into a house. It had seven men in it. There was food on the table and purple haze was in the air. jaBrill asked Jack would he like a drink or something to eat. Jack said, "Sure, I haven't eaten all day." jaBrill went into the kitchen to get some plates. While he was in there, he told one of his men to get the basement ready, to put plastic down over the rug so blood wouldn't get all over it. jaBrill walked back into the dining room with a fake smile and some plates. He began fixing Jack something to eat. When his man passed him some haze, jaBrill took two long puffs, and tried to pass it to Jack.

Jack declined, saying "I'm good, smoking is not my thing."

jaBrill looked puzzled. "What, you don't smoke?"

"No, I don't, my twist is pancakes and syrup, and since you have invited me to your get-together, and I didn't bring anything, I got something for us." Jack reached in his bag, and pulled out a gallon of blueberry tusk, and over 200 pancakes (or zanexes, for your niggas reading this book that don't know what pancakes are). jaBrill and his hommies' eyes lit the fuck up. Jack said, "It should be enough in the bottle to get us all fucked up."

jaBrill said, "Damn, I might have to let this nigga live."

Jack said, "As a matter of fact, you all drink this, I got my own little personal bottle."

jaBrill said, "Damn!" Them niggas dived right in.

See what Jack had in his bottle wasn't syrup. Jack started acting like he was nodding, telling jaBrill he had more where that came from. jaBrill was still going to take him for everything he was worth, but right now, the blueberry tusk was tasting too good. Jack stumbled over to the couch and sat down, playing possum by pretending that he was sleep. For the next eight hours, them niggas ate all those pancakes and drank all that syrup. They were all fucked up. That shit Jack had in that bottle was sweet and strong. Jack laid there for a few more hours, until he didn't hear any more noise, just niggas snoring. Jack got up and looked at everybody lying all over the place, higher than a mother fucker—jaBrill and all seven of his men. Jack grabbed his bookbag and zipped open the front pouch, pulled out a pair of black gloves and put them on. Then he picked all of them niggas up and lined all of them up on the floor in front of the couch. He pulled out Norm and twisted a silencer on the front of him; he pulled out Norma and twisted a silencer on the front of her. He stood in front of the couch and unloaded on all of them. Norm was spitting *poppoppoppop pop pop*; Norma was spitting *poppoppoppop pop pop*. Niggas' bodies were jerking. Blood shot all over the place, brains were getting blown out, and they didn't even know what was happening to them. Then Jack walked over and stood on top of jaBrill, pointed Norm and Norma right at his chest, and let him have it. *poppop pop pop pop pop pop pop pop poppop pop pop poppop pop pop pop poppop poppop pop pop*, "Now, that was for me," then he reloaded and emptied both clips again. "And that was for Rudy Ray." Jack grabbed his bookbag, put it across his shoulder and left. He had one down and one more stinken mother fucker to go.

CHAPTER 9

Pooh Bear, Leak, and Joe Hot were all at Ra Ra's house. Ra Ra had his first-aid kit patching up Leak's left arm. He got grazed by one of the bullets.

Joe Hot said, "Man, this shit has gotten out of hand, Pooh Bear we got to do something, next time they might kill one of us."

"Ok, you right, but we must be smart about it. Is any of yall trying to go to jail for the rest of your life?"

Leak said, "Man fucked that, I'm going to blast on them niggas as soon as I see anyone of them, it's on-site."

"Now, that's what we need not to be doing," Pooh Bear replied, "we going to get them, but not now, it's extremely too hot."

Joe Hot and Leak weren't trying to hear nothing Pooh Bear was saying. Their minds were made up. Ra Ra finally got a chance to call Sheema back. She asked him if he was busy because she really needed to talk to him.

"No, I'm not busy, but what's up?"

"Man, tell your friends to shut up, they are too loud in my ear."

Ra Ra told Sheema to hold on, and then went outside and sat on the steps. "Now, is that better?"

"Yes, much better."

"Well, Sheema, what's up, are you ok?"

"Well, um…"

"Well, what, Sheema?"

"Ra Ra, I'm pregnant."

"You are, are you sure?"

"Yes, I'm sure, I told you not to be busting all up in me like that. What are we going to do?"

Ra Ra didn't believe in abortions, even though he had six baby mamas. She was just going to have to be number seven. "You do plan on keeping it, don't you?"

"Yes, that's what I planned on doing. You're not mad at me, are you, Ra Ra?"

Pooh Bear came to the door to see if everything was alright. Ra Ra told Sheema to hold on again. "Yes Pooh Bear, I'm good, I will be in in a second." Pooh Bear closed the screen door and went back inside the house. "Hello, Sheema are you there?"

"Yes, I'm here."

"Look Sheema, I'm not mad at you and I promise to be there for you and the baby."

Sheema was happy that Ra Ra wasn't dissing her. She knew that all she had to do was stop being a whore and start being a mother, and Ra Ra would be there for them. "Ra Ra, I have a doctor's appointment in two weeks, will you go with me?"

"Of course, just remind me the day before." Ra Ra and Sheema finished their conversation and hung up. Ra Ra got up and went back in the house with the rest of his boys.

Back at the hospital, Deena was sitting there reading a book to Rudy Ray, when there was a knock at the door. It was her church chaplain. He asked her if she would mind if he said a prayer for Rudy Ray. She said, "No, no I don't mind at all." The chaplain held Rudy Ray's hand and told Deena to bow her head, then he began his prayer: Our Father in Heaven, let us honor your name, bring down your kingdom so you can be worshipped on earth, as you are worshipped in Heaven, and lead us from temptation, and away from evil . . ." as the chaplain continued to pray, Deena just zoned right out, thinking about all the good times that her and Rudy Ray had. And the day he asked her to marry him . . . the chaplain tapped her, bringing her back from her daydream. He said, "All together now, in Jesus' name we pray, amen."

"Thirty-four, thirty-five, thirty-six, thirty-seven thousand dollars, honey, that's how much money we have in our safe, and the store is doing really good numbers, also. The ATM machine ran out of money today and it took Brinks all day long to come and refill it, oh, and Deena called, she said that Rudy Ray squeezed her hand today." Jack was glad to hear that. He never went to the hospital to see Rudy Ray because he didn't want to see him like that, but he told Deena to keep him posted about Rudy Ray's condition, and to notify him if he wakes up. Jack could hear that mom Parker was talking to him, but his mind was on killing Kato.

Pooh Bear, Leak, and Joe Hot were sitting around Carmen's house cracking your-mama jokes on each other. Carmen told them that their jokes was so corny that you had to laugh. Chippy and Mya were laughing at everything.

Joe Hot told Leak that "Your mom is so old, that she got rock letters on her birth certificate," then Leak said, "Joe Hot, your mom is so fat, that she used a VCR for a beeper," everybody fell out laughing.

Pooh Bear told Chippy that "her mom house was so small, that he threw a rock in the door, and hit everybody."

Mya said, "Shut up, Pooh Bear, because your mom is so dumb, she put a peephole in a glass door."

"You stupid, your mom so dumb, that when we was at the mall, she opened her new phone, and when she turned it on, she just took off running, and when I finally caught up with her, I said why did you start running, she said because when I looked at my phone, it said sprint." Oh shit, yall simple mother fuckers got my stomach hurting. Now that was some funny shit.

"Shut up Leak that's why your mom so cross-eyed, that when she cries, the tears roll down her back."

They were all having a ball, the most fun that any of them had in a long time. Then Pooh Bear got a text message and didn't know who it was from, but it said, "Footty, E-money, Day Day, and Apple were all out in Tasker at some girl named Sabrina's house, getting high on her front steps." Pooh Bear showed the text to his boys, they had a small discussion, then told Carmen that they would be back.

Footty and E-money were talking to Sabrina and her sister, while Day Day and Apple were rolling up some dutches, as they were smoking on some black and miles. Pooh Bear and his crew slid right up on them.

"Yo Footty, let me holler at you, dog."

"Man, only thing you can do is holler at this dick, nigga."

Leak and Joe Hot went right in on Apple and Day Day. Pooh Bear stole E-money, knocking him straight the fuck out. Then Footty stole Pooh Bear, they locked ass again, but this time Footty was high, and Pooh Bear was winning. Leak and Joe Hot were stomping the shit out of Apple and Day Day, them niggas got caught high, trippen,' and slippen.' Footty's mouth was all busted open and his nose was bleeding. Footty was throwing wild haymakers and Pooh Bear was dipping them, hitting him with precision combinations. This one was getting ugly. Sabrina ran in the house and grabbed a ten-inch-butcher knife, and gave it to Footty, and Footty started swinging it at Pooh Bear. Now he had the upper hand. Pooh Bear pulled off his shirt so he could try to catch the knife. He knew that if Footty stabbed him with that big ass knife it would be over. Carmen got a call telling her Footty was trying to stab Pooh Bear. She dropped the phone and grabbed a hammer. Her and her girlfriends ran to the fight. Footty came with the overhand stab, Pooh Bear dodged it and punched him right in his eye. Footty was seeing stars. Pooh Bear then rushed him and grabbed his hand with the knife in it, wrapped his shirt around it and pulled it tight. They started tussling. Sabrina screamed and told Footty to get him. Pooh Bear held on to Footty's hand for dear life; one slip and he would be dead. Pooh Bear started banging Footty's hand against the parked car's side-view mirror, until he dropped the knife. He then grabbed him and flipped him over on to the ground and fell on top of him. Footty tried to bite Pooh Bear, but Pooh Bear just kept on rearranging his face. Carmen ran up and gave Pooh Bear the hammer. He grabbed Footty by the face and turned his head to the side, then raised the hammer with the forks side up, bringing it down for the kill. Just as the hammer was about to hit Footty's head, Ra Ra grabbed his arm and said, "No, Pooh Bear you are going to jail." Ra Ra got there in the nick of time because Pooh Bear would have killed Footty. Footty got up and told Pooh Bear that his days were numbered. As him and his boys ran off, Carmen and her girls were checking on Pooh Bear and his hommies to make sure they were alright. When Mya noticed that Leak had blood all over the back of his shirt, they first thought that it was from Apple or Day Day, until Leak collapsed a few minutes later. It looked like Footty wasn't the only one with a knife; Apple had one, too.

Carmen, Sheema, Mya, and Chippy were coming from Pathmark on Graysferry Avenue getting them some girly stuff, when they saw Sabrina walking down Twenty-Ninth and Reed, so they decided to follow her, Sabrina continued to walk down until she hit Thirty-Second and Reed, eventually going into Stinger Square Park. She went over to the play area where the swings were, and the children were playing. Carmen was like "I hope this bitch don't think because she's over there with those children, that her ass is safe, that shit she did the other night, I'm going to kick her ass for it."

They all walked over to where Sabrina was sitting at, "What's up, bitch?"

"Nothing much. Please Carmen, I don't want any trouble."

"You should've thought about that before you tried to get Pooh Bear hurt."

"But Carmen?"

"Shut up, bitch," smacking her in the face. The little kids started running out of the play area. Carmen smacked her again, Chippy grabbed her by her hair, and Mya kicked her in her ass. Sheema stepped to the side and out of the way.

"Please stop, I'm so sorry."

Mya kicked her in her ass again. Chippy had a handful of her hair and banged her face against the monkey bars. That opened a gash right underneath her eye. Sabrina fell to the ground, and they all started stomping her, everybody except Sheema. When they were finished, Sabrina was all messed up, laying on the ground in a puddle of blood. Regretting going against the grain by helping Footty, she knew she was from Tasker and that's where her loyalty should have been. Mya was asking Sheema why she didn't help them beat that bitch ass. Sheema kept quiet.

Chippy was like, "Did you see how I banged that bitch face against those monkey bars?"

Carmen said, "Yes, and I smacked the bitch like she owed me something." Sheema gave a fake laugh, and everybody knew it was fake. "Girl what the fuck is wrong with you?" As a tear rolled down Sheema's face.

"Hold up, I know you not upset because we kicked that bitch ass?"

"No, it's nothing."

"It's gotta be something because you didn't even help us."

Sheema said, "Well, it's not like I didn't want to, I just couldn't."

"What do you mean you couldn't?"

"I just couldn't."

"No, there is no you couldn't."

"You're going to tell us right now what is going on, or we are going to beat your ass."

"Okay but that wouldn't be a good idea."

"And why not?"

Sheema took a deep breath, "Because . . ."

"Because what, spit it out?"

"Okay fuck it, I'm pregnant."

All the girls stopped walking and said at the same time, "Pregnant? Pregnant by who?"

"Yall won't believe it, it's Ra Ra's, remember that day we had that orgy?"

"Yes."

"Well, that's when it must have happened."

"Girl no you didn't let that nigga bust all up in you, are you crazy, don't you know everybody that Ra Ra sleeps with without a condom, he gets them pregnant? Shit girl, which makes you baby momma number seven."

"Yes, is that bad?"

"No, not if he takes care of yall."

"Man, I would give anything for Pooh Bear to knock me the fuck up. I love that nigga to death, but I guess right now, we will just have to settle for your baby." They all hugged Sheema and told her that everything was going to be okay.

Three weeks later, Leak was about all healed up from the incident where Apple had stabbed him. Joe Hot wanted to get at them niggas for what they did to his man.

Joe Hot told Leak, "Man we can't let this shit ride, them niggas gotta pay for what they did to you."

Leak said, "But Pooh Bear said—"

"Man, fuck what Pooh Bear said. You in or out?"

"I'm in, nigga, what you think." They began putting their plans together.

Meanwhile, on the other side of South Philadelphia, Duck and Jack was talking. "Yo, what is up my nigga, which was some real crafty shit you pulled down on Seventh Street, nobody have any idea who took jaBrill out, all they know is whoever did it got some real fucken balls."

"You know what Duck, fuck jaBrill, he had it is coming and Kato do to. I have forty-two fucken bullets with his name on it."

Duck told his bartender to give him another drink. "Look Jack, speaking of Kato, I hear he got a graduation he is supposed to be attending. It will be at Dobbins High School on Twenty-Second and Lehigh. I think his nephew is graduating." Jack and Duck continued their conversation, then Jack thanked him again and left.

As Leak finished passing the screwdrivers to Joe Hot, Joe Hot told him to be on watch for the cops, Joe Hot was stealing a black Impala for their mission in hand. Five minutes later they were cruising away. Their destination was the Wilson Park projects. Leak and Joe Hot were slow driving through Wilson looking for Footty and his crew. they went up and down each street and seen not one of them. So they rode up to the nearest 7-Eleven and got some dutches and Black and Milds. Leak brought a couple of scratch-off tickets and hit for twenty dollars. He cashed the ticket in, got back in the car, and headed back to Wilson. Sitting outside on the steps was Apple. He was talking to some chick.

Joe Hot said, "Yo, there go one of those niggass right there." Joe Hot proceeded to tell Leak to circle back around the block. Leak did just what Joe Hot told him to do, speeding the car up until he got back around to where Apple was.

Leak slowed the car down in front of him, saying, "Yo player, who got some of that chronic around here?" Apple just looked at them and kept talking to the girl.

Joe Hot screamed out, "What's up Apple, how have you been?"

Apple said, "Who is that?"

"It's me hommie. Oh, so, now you don't know who I am?"

Apple walked a little closer to see who it was, putting his hand near his waist, not knowing Leak already had his 40-caliber weapons to the car door. Apple replied, "I said, who is that cuz?"

When he finally realized who it was, it was too late. *block ah, block ah,* Leak hit him twice, right through the car door, and Apple went down. Then Leak pulled off.

Joe Hot started yelling at him. "Stop this fucking car right now!"

Leak slammed on the brakes. "What's up Joe?"

"Man, back this car the fuck up right now?" Leak put the car in reverse and backed up. When he got back to Apple, Joe Hot jumped out of the car and ran over to him. Apple was trying to reach for his gun, but his injuries wouldn't let him.

Joe Hot yelled out, "Stab somebody now, motherfucker!" Then he shot him. *Block ah* "Stab somebody now, you bitch ass nigga," then shot him again. *Block ah* Leak was hollering out of the window telling Joe Hot to get back in the car. "Man fuck this nigga, Leak." Then shot him two more times. *Block ah, block ah* Then all Leak saw in his rearview mirror was red and blue spinning lights closing in fast. Joe Hot ran and jumped back into the car and Leak took off. The chases was on. Leak was on the outskirts of the Schoolkill Expressway going well over the speed limit. The cops were on his ass. The cops radioed in for backup. "This is squad car one eighty-seven calling for backup, in pursuit of a black Impala, license plate b,l, e, two,five,six,zero, going well over a hundred miles an hour, headed towards the Tasker projects." Leak made a sharp right turn and almost lost control of the car. As he started sliding to the side, Joe Hot rolled down the window like he was about to give up to the police, then he thought about it, and rolled the window back up. Leak heard sirens coming from all over. Then another police car hit him from the side. *Bam* Leak veered off and hit two parked cars, *Bam, Bam*, but he kept going. Now two cops were on his ass so Leak banged a hard right and went up Natrona Street the wrong way, made a quick left past Audenreid, and continued down the outskirts of the Expressway going towards the bottom. He then hit a sharp left, half three sixty, and hit the Expressway. As he was sliding, the cop rammed the shit out of him from behind. Joe Hot was on his knees in the front car seat, ready to shoot. Leak had the peddle to the metal. Then a light covered the whole entire car from up above. The police helicopter had them locked in. Now it was six cops on the chase. Leak exited off at the Passyunk Avenue exit and went straight through the red light, causing four cars to bang out. He crossed over the medium trying to regain control of the car, going the wrong way up Oregon Avenue. He crossed back over to the right side of the street, and as he approached Broad and Oregon Avenue, he went up onto the sidewalk and into the park, smashing through park benches and tearing up the grass. Then he hit a pile of dirt and the car went airborne. When it landed Leak lost total control of the car, and smashed dead into a tree. Going over a hundred miles an hour, Leak went face first into the steering wheel crushing his skull and upper chest, killing him instantly. And the force from the crash threw Joe Hot through the front windshield about ten feet away from the car, severing his arm which landed about two feet away from his body. The police got out and ran over to the boys. They radioed in for fire rescue and then tried to handcuff Joe Hot, until they notice one of his arms was missing. Fire rescue got there within minutes and pronounced Leak dead on the scene. Joe Hot was unconscious, but still alive. The paramedics put Joe Hot on a stretcher, and put him and his arm in the back of the ambulance headed for Methodist Hospital. The EMTs put an oxygen mask over Joe Hot's face then gave him a Thorazine shot and wrapped his arm to stop the bleeding. Joe Hot's heart rate kept rising. The paramedics were working so hard to stop Joe Hot from going into shock, but the efforts were in vain. Joe Hot flatlined. They started CPR right away; one, two, three, breathe, one, two, three, breathe, one, two, three, breathe. . . Joe Hot's eyes began to roll in the back of his head. It was over. He was dead and so was Leak.

The next morning, word was spreading fast that Joe Hot and Leak killed Apple, and then they were killed trying to get away from the police in a hot-pursuit chase. Ra Ra called Pooh Bear and Pooh Bear's phone just kept ringing. "Come on, Pooh Bear, pick the phone up, please pick up." Ra Ra hung up and called back. Pooh Bear was in the shower and couldn't hear his phone ringing. So Ra Ra hung up and left out of his door and started running all the way to Pooh Bear's house. Pooh Bear got out of the shower and was drying off when he heard Ra Ra calling him and whistling up at his bedroom window. He looked out of the window and told Ra Ra to hold on. Pooh Bear put his clothes on so that he could go and see what was going on. When he opened the door, Ra Ra was just standing there, his cheeks were all red, with tears rolling down from his eyes.

"Tell me it's not true, Pooh Bear."

"Tell you what is not true, what the hell are you talking about?"

"You mean to tell me you haven't heard?"

"Heard what?"

"That Leak and Joe Hot got killed last night."

"Ra Ra what the fuck are you talking about?" Pooh Bear started getting emotional. What Ra Ra was saying couldn't possibly be true, but it was.

Footty, E-money, and Day Day were all at the county morgue with Apple's parents. As they were identifying his body, Apple's mom couldn't believe she was looking at her only son, laying on a cold-ass table dead with no life in his body. Apple's dad was holding her as they both were crying. Footty walked over to her and said he was sorry for their loss. Apple's mom lifted her head, looked at him, then spit in his face. She said, "It was all your fault that my son is dead, and if he was never following after you, he would still be alive." Footty knew just how she was feeling because he had just buried his own mother. E-money and Day Day told Footty to come on and go, and they would take it out on them niggas out in Tasker.

CHAPTER 10

J ack's patience was wearing thin. He wanted Kato, but he would not
move. Kato stayed in the Passyunk projects and wouldn't come out.
Jack was thinking he would have to go in and get him. He knew Passyunk
was like a fortress. There were many who went in, but only a few that ever
came back out. So, he just continued to play like he was a bum, sitting on
the A+ store steps, begging for quarters so he could keep an eye on the
way those Passyunk niggas were moving.

A week later, the church bells were ringing as everybody was making
their way to their seats for Joe Hot and Leak's funeral. Joe Hot and Leak's
parents decided to give the two boys a funeral together, since they grew
up together as best friends. In the front of the church were two beautiful
white-and-gold-trimmed coffins, with Leak on one side and Joe Hot on the
other. Joe Hot just looked like he was sleeping; he had on a light-blue-
double-breasted-sharkskin suit, with blue gators to match. Leak had on a
three-piece-Brooks-Brothers suit with a black pair of Stacy Adams. He
also had a white net covering the front of his coffin so you couldn't really
see all the damage that was done to his face. Pooh Bear, Ra Ra, Carmen,
Sheema, Mya, and Chippy all stood in front of their coffins crying and
touching Leak and Joe Hot not believing they were gone. The whole

church was filled with tears and sadness. Joe Hot's mom could barely stand. Leak's parents were still in shock that their baby boy had crossed over, and it was nothing they could do about it. The boys were gone forever. The preacher came up to the pulpit and started to preach. "It is unfortunate today that we are gathered here to celebrate the death of two young men, tragically taken from this world before their time. They were somebodies' sons, somebodies' brothers, and even somebodies' fathers. The world can be cruel, then we must die, we must try to hold back our tears, and rejoice. See the world is backwards. Let me explain why I'm saying that. People, you are supposed to cry when a baby is born into a world of sin and celebrate when a person leaves this world to have eternal life. Joseph Hall and Maleak Davis didn't die, they have just moved on to the spiritual world where we will soon follow. For as we are born, we shall surely die. The body that is, not your spirit. I believe Joseph and Maleak are in Heaven looking down on us right now. The bodies you see here in front of you are just houses they used to live in, now they live with God." What the preacher was saying made a lot of sense, but it didn't stop anybody from crying. Pooh Bear and Ra Ra were crying just as hard as the ladies, but Ra Ra would never be the same. As the pastor finished up, the next segment was a tribute to the boys. As the music started to play, all you could hear was the most beautiful voice you've ever heard coming from the back of the church. It was Philly's own Patty LaBelle. She was singing "His Eye is on the Sparrow," and she was bringing down the church. See Patty LaBelle had heard about the young boys' deaths while she was in town, and wanted to do something for the family, so she sung for the boys free of charge. After she finished her song, she left out the back with her security. The pastor said, "We will now have the obituary readings by Miss Carmen Jackson. Carmen got up with tears running down her face. She opened the obituaries and went to read them, but when she spoke, nothing came out. Joe Hot's mom said, "It's okay baby, take your time." Carmen got herself together and took a deep breath and began to read, "Joseph Darrell Hall was born January 10, 1989, to Trenda Mitchell, and Joseph Darrell Hall Senior, who has preceded him in death. He was educated at Alcorn Elementary and South Philadelphia High School where he did not graduate but was about to obtain his GED. He was a very fun person and even better friend to be around, he loved everybody, and everybody loved him." Joe Hot's mom was looking at the pictures of her son, smiling and so full of life in the obituary. The one that stuck out the most was the one where she was holding him as a baby. It was just too much for her to bear. She jumped up and ran to Joe Hot's coffin and laid on his chest crying her heart out. The preacher and the deacons just let her get it out of her system. Mya, Chippy, and Sheema were holding each other, sobbing. Pooh Bear and Ra Ra were telling each other that everything was going to be okay. Carmen finished up reading all the poems that were on the back then cried some more as she went back to her seat. Then Pooh Bear got up and took the microphone. "Hello family and friends today is a sad day, and I would like to read you something I wrote for my friends. Joe Hot and Leak, I stand here and speak, you were so full of life and so upbeat, it breaks my heart to see yall here, as I used all my strength, to hold back my tears, I wish you could get up, and give me some dap, but unfortunately, it doesn't work like that, you all my friends, and you were so close to me, I must accept the fact, that you are now free, time will tell every story, and your stories have been told, I wish to God, he would have let y'all grow old . . ." just as Pooh Bear looked up, he saw Footty, E-money, and Day Day walking into the church. Everybody turned around and looked. The ushers told them to be quiet and have a seat. They sat right behind Joe Hot and Leak's parents. Pooh Bear thought "Why is these niggas here?" Ra Ra reached in his waist, but nothing was there. Footty and his crew stood up and walked to the center of the room and threw a whole bunch of papers all over the floor. Then left. The ushers started picking up the papers, noticing that they were obituaries. And all of them were the same. They said, "The homegoing of Aaron Baker, A.K.A. Apple: Sunrise May 8, 1989, Sunset September 19, 2007."

As Mya, Chippy, Sheema, and Carmen were riding back from the funeral home, Carmen was really upset, thinking about how it easily could have been Pooh Bear. Sheema got dropped off at Ra Ra's house, then Chippy got dropped off at home. The limo driver was dropping Carmen off next, when she dropped her head into her hands and started crying again, knowing that the Tasker and Wilson beef was not over. Pooh Bear was caught up in the middle of it. The limo driver got to Carmen's house and let her out, she was walking and almost fell. Mya got out to help her and told the driver that he could go ahead and leave. Mya helped Carmen to the door as she could not stop crying. Pooh Bear was all she kept thinking about. Carmen and Mya entered the house, and she went straight to the phone and called Pooh Bear, but his voice-messaging service picked up. She put the phone down and told Mya she was scared for her man. Mya told Carmen not to worry, that Pooh Bear knew how to take care of himself. A few minutes later, Pooh Bear called Carmen back. After they finished talking, Carmen hung up and began crying even harder.

Mya said, "Stop crying Carmen, what did he say?"

"He said he couldn't let Footty, and his crew get away with what they started."

Mya got up and hugged Carmen telling her everything was going to be alright. Carmen laid in Mya's arms and chest and cried like a baby. Mya felt a surge of heat hit her between her legs, and her moist pussy started twitching. Mya started rubbing on Carmen's back.

"Don't worry Carmen, I'm here for you."

As she began to rub the side of her hair, Carmen started to feel a little strange, especially when Mya's nipples got hard, pressing up against her face. Carmen tried to pull away, but Mya held onto her tightly. She looked down at Carmen's face, then started wiping away her tears. Carmen went to say something, then Mya kissed her right in her mouth. Carmen pushed her away, then Mya kissed her again, and again. Then Carmen finally kissed her back. Mya started sticking her tongue all in Carmen's mouth and biting down on her bottom lip. Carmen's pussy was on fire and her panties were soaking wet. Mya pulled off her shirt and bra and let her beautiful, brown titties and fat nipples bounce through the air. Carmen took one of Mya's breasts and put it in her mouth. Mya closed her eyes as Carmen sucked and rolled her tongue around the tip of her nipples. Mya's vagina came in seconds. Carmen couldn't believe what she was doing, but she was too excited to stop. Mya unbuttoned the back of Carmen's dress. Then she slid her arms out and let the dress hit the floor. Mya always wanted to see Carmen naked, and here she was, standing in front of her with just her see-through panties and bra. Mya couldn't believe how fat Carmen's pussy was, not to mention she had a fat camel toe sticking through her panties. Mya walked over and put her hand between Carmen's gap and squeezed it while gently pinching on her nipples. Carmen moaned, and started to grind against Mya's hand, which was completely covered in her juices. Mya reached behind Carmen, popped her bra, and took it off. Then Carmen said, "Get down on the couch," and Mya got between her legs and started to kiss her all over her neck, licking her from the top of her chest down to her belly button, then back up to her breasts. Carmen spread her legs and begged Mya to take her panties off. Mya slid Carmen's panties off and exposed her pretty twat and extremely huge clit. The panties Mya had in her hands were full of cream. Carmen grabbed Mya by her head and smashed her face between her legs. Mya put her tongue on Carmen's clit and began to lick and suck her pussy. Carmen was going wild. Mya put part of Carmen's clit between her teeth and gently began to slurp. Then she put her legs high into the air. As her toes began to curl, Carmen pumped Mya's face like she was getting some dick. Mya couldn't breathe as Carmen was smashing her pussy into her face. The bottom half of Mya's face was covered in pure-white come. Mya started licking Carmen's pussy faster and faster. Carmen humped harder and harder. Mya had to come up for air, and when she did, Carmen commenced to kissing Mya rough in the mouth, licking her own pussy juices off Mya's face. Mya told Carmen to calm down, then stood up and took her own panties off and began to play with herself as she pulled on her nipple piercings. Mya started shaking hard as she began to come herself. Carmen's mouth was watering for the taste of Mya's twat. And then Mya came. Carmen got down on her knees and started to kiss Mya all over her inner thighs.

Mya grabbed a handful of Carmen's hair and said, "Now lick this pussy, bitch," and Carmen started to lick. Mya smacked her and told her to slow down. "I like when you slow lick this pussy, do you understand me?"

Carmen said, "Yes."

Mya fell back in the recliner and Carmen didn't miss a lick. This was the first time she was eating some pussy, and she was doing it like a pro. Mya told Carmen to put her tongue in her pussy hole and blow air into it. Carmen again did what she said, Mya's pussy started to fart, then Carmen stuck her finger in her ass. Mya jumped a little bit but didn't tell Carmen to stop. Carmen was jamming her finger into Mya's ass and blowing air into her pussy. Mya couldn't even talk; it was feeling so good. She just continued to smack the side of Carmen's face. Mya started shaking again, and then wrapped her legs around Carmen's head so tight that Carmen had no choice but to drink her pussy come that Mya was leaking into her mouth. Carmen got up and Mya laid on the floor. Carmen sat down on her face pumping her pussy up and down and rubbing it back and forth. Mya was in heaven. She slid Carmen off of her face and turned her around backwards to put her face between her ass cheeks. Carmen didn't know that you could come from your ass, but she was about to find out. Her left leg started to get weak and her stomach tightened up. As her ass busted for the first time, Carmen screamed out telling Mya she never felt anything like that before. Mya knew she was turning Carmen out. Carmen fell to her back, out of breath, but Mya wasn't finish yet. Mya got down between Carmen's legs and went back to work. This time she put the whole clit into her mouth and gently sucked it. Carmen started beating on the floor and grabbing onto the carpet, like when Pooh Bear ate her pussy. Mya wanted her to squirt for her like she did for him. And Carmen was about to let it go. She was begging for Mya to stop, but Mya wasn't having it. She knew Carmen was close so she licked faster and sucked a little harder. It was only minutes before Carmen popped. The come started shooting out like a sprinkler. Mya lay right there and never moved; she was washing her face in it; it was shooting all in her mouth, her hair, and up her nose. When Carmen was done coming, Mya just laid the side of her face down on top of Carmen's wet pussy, and then they both just fell asleep.

Early the next morning, Footty and his crew were talking. "Yo E-money, we should have blasted on them niggas, for real. I don't give a fuck that we were at no funeral, them faggot's killed Apple."

"Footty, the one's that killed Apple are dead, so why would you want to shoot up a church? That doesn't make any sense."

"Man, shut the fuck up, Day Day, or else."

"Or else what?"

"Or else I'm going to bust a cap in your ass."

"Oh, so you're going to shoot me now? Man, you are trippin'."

"No, both of y'all are tripping. If anything, we should be mad at them Tasker bitches, not each other. So put away your gun, Footty, like you were really about to shoot Day Day. What tip is you on?"

"Man, who the fuck yall bitch-ass niggas thinks you talking to? What, do y'all forget who the leader of this crew is?"

"Look dog, we are going to holler at you later because right now you are in your bag." E-money and Day Day rolled out. Footty was really going to shoot Day Day. He was really starting not to give a fuck who he killed. Somebody is going to half to die.

At the hospital, Deena was sitting next to Rudy Ray's bed watching As the World Turns when mom Parker walked in, asking her how was Rudy doing. "He is doing good, I just got through feeding him and giving him a bath."

"Good, now let's get out of this hospital and do some shopping." Deena was glad mom Parker came by. She had been at the hospital ever since Rudy Ray got shot and needed to get some air.

"Okay, let me get myself together. You know a bitch gotta look good." A few minutes later, Deena came out of the bathroom ready to go. She then told the doctors and the nurses that she was leaving and would be back later. Deena and mom Parker went down on the elevator.

"Shit girl, before we go anywhere, I need to get my ass something to eat. My stomach is touching my back." So they stopped at the lunch truck outside of University Hospital. "Miss, can I please have a meatball sandwich with parmesan cheese and extra sauce, with a Caesar salad, a bag of chips, and a Pepsi."

"Damn bitch, what you pregnant or something?"

"No girl, I just haven't eaten all day."They both got some food, then walked away laughing, until they reached mom Parker's car. Then they got in and left.

"Yo E-money, I think that nigga really was going to shoot me."

"Me too, Day Day, I don't trust him like that anymore. Should we kill him first, before he kills one of us?"

"Naw, I don't think we got to do that, he was just taking Apple's death really hard. And you know his mom just not too long ago passed away, we just need to fall back for a couple of days and give him some space, and in a couple of days, if he is still acting the same way, I will kill him myself."

Ra Ra was sitting at the table with his gun loaded, thinking real crazy when the house phone rang. "Hello, you have a call from the Youth Study Center, from Bay Boy, if you accept this call, please press five." Ra Ra hit number five and began to talk to Bay Boy. "What's up my nigga?"

"What's up Ra Ra?"

"I'm chillin,' man, can't wait to get the fuck out of here."

"I know, we need you. Shit about to get real dark for the niggas in Wilson. I'm not playing anymore games."

"Well, what about Pooh Bear?"

"Shit, he's not letting this shit slide, either, or he got something major for you when you come home."

"Word?"

"Word."

"That's what's up. Ra Ra, please tell me you didn't knock Sheema up."

"I sure did. Why? I didn't know the pussy was so good, I forgot I didn't have a condom on."

"Ra Ra, don't get me wrong, she is beautiful and all, but you know she been around the block."

"I know, but she is my baby mama now, and you can't talk about her like that."

"Alright, my bad, I can respect that— "you now have sixty seconds"—

"Damn dog, how much time do they give you in there?"

"Only ten minutes a day, but I used five minutes of it earlier. I will have to holler at you another time ..." then the phone hung up.

"Now you know them pants is too damn tight."

"Shut up, no they are not." Both girls laughed.

"If Rudy Ray knew you had those tight-ass pants on, he would wake up and tell you to take them off."

"You think so? In that case, I'll take two pair."

"Stop playing girl, if these pants gonna wake Rudy up, don't you think I should buy two of them?"

"No I don't, plus they might rip by the time you get back to the hospital."

"Ha ha, very funny, I wasn't going to buy those tight-ass jeans anyway, I was just fucking with you."

Deena brought two shirts and some panties, and a bottle of perfume before they left the store. As they continued to walk downtown, they passed a porno store on Twelfth and Market. "Hold up Tina, I got to go in here. Shit, I haven't had any dick in months." Deena went into the porno store and mom Parker went next door, to the dollar store. Deena was looking around, then the sales guy came over to ask her if she need any help. Deena told him exactly what she wanted and he pointed her in the right direction. Twenty minutes later, mom Parker walked into the porno store where Deena was shopping. Deena was at the cash register, getting her items rung up. She bought two porno DVDs; one was "How the Big Dicks Won the West"; the other one was "How the Even Bigger Dicks Won the South". Tina could do nothing but laugh, knowing Deena was about to get her shit off, as soon as she got home.

CHAPTER 11

Jack was walking around in the Passyunk projects dressed like a bum. He was dirty and was pushing around a shopping cart with trash in it. He had gotten a tip on the house where he could find Kato. Jack moved into position and knocked on the door. As he waited for somebody to answer, he started eating out of the trash. One of Kato's bodyguards came to the door. When he opened it, all he saw was a bum eating out of the trash. He then yelled out, "Get the fuck away from here!" while kicking Jack in his ass. Jack fell over the trashcan and just lay there. The bodyguards shut the door and went back into the house. Twenty minutes later, the bodyguard came back to the door and Jack was still laying on the ground not moving. "Oh shit, did I just kill this motherfucker? If I did, he got to get the fuck away from this house." As the bodyguard bent over to see if Jack was dead, Jack pulled his gun and shot him between his eyes. Bone and brain matter shot straight up into the air. Then Jack rolled out of the way so the bodyguard didn't fall on top of him. Jack got up and twisted the silencer on Norma a little bit tighter. He then slowly pushed the door open and could see another bodyguard sitting on the couch watching TV. Jack slid in the house, posted up against the kitchen wall, then slid into the heater closet, got down on his knees, and crawled over to the back of the sofa where the bodyguard was sitting. Jack reached up, grabbed home boy around his neck, then shot him through his back four times. Jack heard somebody coming down the steps so he hid behind a wall. As soon as the poor bastard turned the corner, Jack put one in the side of his head. He didn't know what hit him. Jack crept up the steps with Norm and Norma in both hands. He then peeked into the front room. It was two people in there fucking. Jack walked up to both of them, as this nigga was hitting that ass from the back. He pointed Norma at her head and Norm at his head, then pulled the trigger. That nigga died in mid stroke, as both of their bodies fell over to the side shaking. Jack then heard somebody in the bathroom. He quickly ducked down behind the door. Somebody was in the bathroom asking for one of his hommies to bring him some toilet paper. He kept sticking his hand out of the door waiting for it. Jack reached up on the shelf and grabbed the roll of paper then handed it to him. "Damn," he said, "what the fuck took yall niggas so long to give me some tissue so I can wipe my ass?" Jack didn't answer, he just waited for him to clean himself up. When Jack heard the toilet flush, he kicked open the door. This nigga got caught with his pants down, literally. Jack pushed him into the tub, then hit him from the waist up. He could have at least let the man pull his pants up, but he didn't. Jack felt a little sense of relief, until he checked all of the bodies and found out not one of them was Kato. Jack pushed his cart back over to the A+ store and finished begging for quarters for the rest of the day, wondering how the fuck did he miss his target.

Pooh Bear lay in his room. His mind was pondering on what his next move was going to be. He wished this whole situation would just go away, but he knew it would never happen as long as Footty was still living. Joe Hot and Leak killed Apple, and Footty wanted revenge. He wasn't going to stop until he got either Ra Ra or Pooh Bear. So Pooh Bear and Ra Ra were going to have to get him first. But when and how were the big questions. Pooh Bear thought so hard about it that he soon dozed off and fell asleep. Jack got a call from Duck telling him that he had something he needed, but he had to come right away and bring ten thousand dollars with him. Jack was puzzled. "What the fuck do Duck want me to bring that kind of money with me? Something must be up, and if it is, Duck's gonna get

94

it, too." Jack didn't fully trust anyone, except his wife, Tina, so now Duck was on his radar. Jack went home, opened his safe, and got the money. He started walking to Duck's house, checking out everything. Nothing seemed strange or out of place, so he knocked on the door. Duck soon answered it, shook Jack's hand, and gave him a hug.

"What's going on, Jack?"

"Nothing much, I'm chillin.' Now what is this about, what do you have for me that I needed to bring this kind of money?"

Duck just smiled, then said, "Now Jack, how long have we known each other?"

"A long fucking time, Duck, now get to your point."

"My point is, you know I am a businessman, right?"

"Okay, so what are you getting at, Duck?"

"All I'm saying is that if you gotten grand, I got something you need." So Jack threw Duck the bag of money, Duck reached in the bag and flicked the pile of money. Knowing it all was there, Duck then pointed to the basement door. Jack looked at the door, then back at Duck, then pulled out Norm. Duck said, "You won't be needing that, everything you need is already down there." Jack still didn't put his gun away. Duck laughed, and said, "Some things never change." Duck knew Jack wanted him to go down first, so he did. When they both got to the bottom of the steps, Duck pointed to the center of the basement. There was a chair with somebody sitting in it with long hair. Duck went back upstairs, turned on the basement lights, told Jack to have fun, then closed the door. Jack checked the basement out to see if anybody else was there, and it wasn't. Jack walked over to the person in the chair with the long hair and bag covering her face. Jack thought to himself, "Who the fuck is this, what kind of game was Duck playing?" The ropes were so tight around her arms, it looked like they were cutting off her circulation. Jack walked over and pulled the bag off of her head, then he jumped back. Like what the fuck? Then he started smiling. It wasn't a girl at all, it was Kato. Kato took one look at Jack and knew his time was up. Tears just swelled up in his eyes, as he dropped his head. Duck had four tables in the basement and they were all filled with all the torture tools in the world, and Jack planned on using every last one of them. Jack took the duct tape from off of Kato's mouth to allow him to speak, but Kato said nothing. Jack then said, "Kato, Kato, what's up, my man, how have you been?" Kato still refused to talk. "I am going to ask you a question, one time, and one time only, who put that hit out on Rudy Ray?" Kato spat in Jack's face and told him to eat a dick. "Eat a dick, really? Okay, I got your eat a dick." Jack went upstairs and asked Duck for a potato peeler. Jack went back downstairs and picked up a rubber mallet off of the table, then he hit Kato on the side of his temple with it. The first hit dazed Kato. The second one put him to sleep. Jack duct taped Kato's mouth closed again, then took off his socks and shoes. Jack then took the potato peeler and scraped all the skin off of the bottom of his feet, then put them down in a full bucket of rubbing alcohol. Kato regained consciousness. Feeling excruciating pain like his feet were on fire, he looked down and started screaming to the top of his lungs, but no one could hear him because his mouth was taped closed. Jack then whacked him in his nose with the rubber mallet telling him to shut the fuck up, then he hit him again so hard, he broke his nose. Blood started leaking all over the place. Kato passed out again. Jack then took the potato peeler and scraped all the skin off both of his hands, then he took a straight razor and cut slices of meat from between his fingers. Jack wrapped a thick rope around the pipe in the ceiling and tied each one of Kato's hands to it. Next, he walked over to the table and grabbed a hammer with a box of tack nails, a fishhook with fishing lines, and took his bloody fingers and put tack nails under each one of his fingernails. Then used the hammer to bang the tech nails deep under his skin. Kato woke up screaming and in pain. Jack knocked him upside his head again with the rubber mallet, knocking him the fuck out for the third time. He pulled the rope and raised Kato's arms above his head; he grabbed the fishing line, threaded it through the fishhook, and sewed Kato's eye lids shut. Small holes were sliced in his armpits and Jack sprayed WD-40 into his wounds. Jack then took Kato's feet out of the pan and onto the floor. He grabbed a nail gun, put six-inch nails into it, then shot nails through each one of his toes, nailing his feet to the floor. Kato was unconscious, but his body was dying. Jack took an electric drill, put a cement-drill bit into it, and placed it onto Kato's knee cap. When he pulled the trigger, the drill cracked his knee right in half; he started drilling on the other one, blood was everywhere. Every time Jack did something to this nigga, he thought about what he had done to Rudy Ray. Kato had holes in his knees, his feet were nailed to the floor, his eyelids were sewn shut, and Jack still wasn't done. Kato's pulse was low, Jack knew he was about to checkout. So, he popped an ammonia pack and put it under his nose. The smell woke Kato up. Jack picked the hammer back up, along with a chisel, then put the chisel on the front of Kato's teeth, raised the hammer, and came down with brute force, breaking Kato's top four teeth and ripping them right out of his gums. Kato swallowed them, choking on his own teeth. Jack then took the rubber mallet and finished beating Kato to death with it. But what Jack didn't know was Duck was sitting back watching and taping the whole thing.

Footty was standing in front of his mom and dad's grave. He buried them next to each other so they would always be with each other. There was a light rain falling on his face as he placed flowers on top of their tombstones. He talked to them, wanting to know why they both left him. It started thundering and lightning. As the rain began to fall harder, Footty looked around and didn't see anyone. It seemed like he was the only one in the whole graveyard. Footty kneeled to say a prayer, and when he was done, he went to get up, and felt something grab his leg, then something grabbed the other one. Footty stood up and tried to run, but there were two hands holding each one of his legs. He tried to pull away, but their grips were too tight. Footty was yelling, but nothing was coming out. He started swinging and punching, but the more he would fight, the deeper he was being pulled into a grave. Then his mother and father both sat up, and he could see their decaying faces. All he kept hearing was, "Come be with us, son." He tried to stay afloat, fighting with all his might, until he was completely pulled under. Then the alarm clock went off, and Footty jumped up in a cold sweat. This was the third time this week that he had the same dream, and it really was bothering him. What did it mean? He felt like he was going to die soon, so some people had to go before he did.

CHAPTER 12

A secret caller, *Ring, Ring*, "Hello."

"Duck, my boy, what's happening?"

"Nothing much, I'm good, what's up?"

"I see Kato turned up in a vacant parking lot out in the middle of the Passyunk projects, tortured to death. You wouldn't know anything about that, now, would you?"

"No, no, not at all, this is the first time I am hearing of it, did you hear who did it?"

"No, but I have a hunch, did you ever relay that information that I gave you to give to BlackJack?"

"I sure did, why?"

"Well, he never showed up to Dobbins to my little set up, me and my men stayed there all day."

"Well, OG Son, you know how crafty he is, maybe he was there, and you just didn't know it."

"You know what, you might be right. Shit, he probably got jaBrill and Kato right under our noses." Both men were highly trained killers, so no average Joe could have taken them out. "You know what, Duck, Jack is becoming a real pain in my ass. Nobody is this fucken hard to kill. Duck, tell me something, do Jack trust you?"

"No not really." Duck was lying.

"Okay, this is what I need you to do. I need you to gain his trust, then kill him, and turn his body over to me."

"Look O.G Son, that's your beef, not mine, I don't want to get involved."

"But Duck, you are already involved, what if Jack was to find out that it was you driving that Yukon, and not jaBrill?" See jaBrill was about to go to war with OG Son, and he needed him out of the way, so he knew, if he implemented jaBrill in the hit on Rudy Ray, Jack would eliminate his problem.

"Damn, is it like that, you never told me that hit was going to be on Jack's best friend?"

"Okay and, do you think Jack is going to give a fuck whether you knew or not?" OG Son was playing dirty, but Duck wasn't about to cross Jack in any conceivable way. He got a firsthand look at what happened to Kato and wanted no parts of it, but he knew how to play the game.

"Alright OG Son, I will see what I can do, I'll keep you posted."

"Yes, you do that Duck, and remember, I am watching you." Duck was caught between a rock and a hard place. That's why he was glad that he taped Jack killing Kato, just in case he had to bargain for his life.

Carmen and Pooh Bear were on Broad and Erie at Black and Nobles picking up copies of the new hood novels that were out. Carmen wanted some Crown Fried Chicken, so they left and walked across the street to eat. Pooh Bear could tell something was wrong with Carmen, but he just couldn't put his finger on it. Carmen was in a good mood, but she wouldn't look him in his face, the guilt was killing her. They did a little more shopping, then got on the subway and headed back to South Philly. As they were riding on the train, Carmen confessed to Pooh Bear what had happened between her and Mya. She told him that Mya had taken advantage of her when she was at her weakest point. She asked if he could he please forgive her. Pooh Bear stood up and looked at her. When the train stopped, he got off, and left her without saying a word.

Ra Ra had Met Sheema at her doctor's appointment just as he had promised. The doctor told Sheema to go into the patient's room and get on the table so that she could give her an ultrasound. Ra Ra sat downright next to her. The nurse came in and put jelly on her belly and rubbed what looked like brush over her stomach. Then a picture of a baby appeared on the monitor. Ra Ra was smiling, until the nurse said, "Wait a minute, I can now here, not one, but two heartbeats." Sheema started crying, thinking something was wrong.

Ra Ra said, "Why do you hear two heartbeats, is something wrong?"

The nurse said, "No, there is no problem, it just means you're going to have twins, congratulations!"

Ra Ra's head started spinning, and Sheema was all smiles. "Man, you got to be kidding me, are they boys or girls?"

The nurse moved a little brush around some more, and said, "Right now I can't tell, but more than likely, on your next visit, we can get a better look."

Sheema got dressed and a nurse gave her her pictures of the ultrasound, along with her next appointment card. She thanked the nurse, and they left. While he was outside flagging down a cab for him and Sheema to get home, he never noticed that Footty had been following them the whole time.

Deena was combing Rudy Ray's hair, getting him ready for the day like she has done ever since he had been in a coma. She had moved into the hospital. The doctors and nurses loved her so to them it didn't even matter. She was feeding Rudy Ray his breakfast. When she noticed he had a hard on underneath the sheets, she smiled and reached underneath his sheets, and said, "Don't worry honey, I'll take it down for you." She gave him a kiss and massaged his manhood, until her hands got wet and sticky.

She then went in the bathroom so she could wash them, and when she returned to his bedside, Rudy Ray was lying there with his eyes wide open.

It had been a nice little while since Footty, E-money, and Day Day had been together. E-money and Day Day was feeling the bad vibe they got that day from Footty, so they fell back just like they said they would. Footty pulled up and blew his horn. E-money and Day Day went over to the car to see what Footty wanted.

"What's the deal, son?" E-money said.

"Nothing much, just wanted to say, my bad, on the other day, I was not myself, I was stressing, and I took it out on my hommies. Can you find it in your heart to forgive me?"

Day Day shook Footty's hand and said "Man, it is all good, ain't no love lost."

E-money shook his hand, too, but he wasn't buying what Footty was selling. He was too polite; in all his years of knowing Footty, he never saw him apologize for anything, there was something behind it, and he was gonna must wait to find out.

"Carmen, you are so dumb, why would you tell Pooh Bear what happened between us?"

"Because I love him, and he won't even talk to me. This is all your fault."

"My fault, I wasn't the only one eating some pussy, you know."

"Oh bitch, no you didn't just go there."

"Bitch, who you calling a bitch?"

"I'm calling you one, how could you do this to me, Mya, I thought you was my friend."

Mya was feeling bad. "I am your friend, Carmen, but I'm also in love with you, too."

"But you know my heart is with Pooh Bear, and although you made me come like crazy, I love me some dick."

"Me too, but I had to have you, I am sorry if I hurt you, but you didn't have to say anything."

"I couldn't lie, he knew something was wrong, it was written all over my face, I couldn't even look him in his eyes."

"Well did you try to call him?"

"I did, but he won't answer none of my calls."

"Look Carmen, I'm going to make this right, even if we both have to sleep with him."

"You really think he would like that?"

"Of course, he would, what man wouldn't?"

"All right then, Mya, thank you, I will talk to you later."

Footty pulled up to the Circle K laundromat where Day Day was chillin,' so he honked the horn and told him to come here for a minute. Day Day ran over to the car, "What's going on, Footty?"

"Nothing much, I just need you to take this ride with me, I know where that sucker-ass Ra Ra live, let's go holler at that nigga."

"Without a doubt, let's ride."

Day Day ran to the other side of the car and got in. "Nice, real nice, where did you get the whip from?"

"I got it from some crackhead, I gave him twenty dollars for the whole night?"

"Word?"

"Word."

Footty and Day Day cruised until they came upon Ra Ra's house. Footty pulled over and parked the car, turned down the radio, and killed the lights. Both could see Ra Ra and Sheema standing in the living room talking. "There goes his bitch ass right there, Day Day. Now, sneak up to the window and bust a cap in his ass."

"And what about the girl?"

"Man fuck her, put one in her ass, too." Day Day got out of the car and snuck up to the window, Ra Ra and sheema was still deep into a discussion. Day Day raised the window and put his fully loaded Mac 10 in position, ready to shoot, then Sheema turned to the side. Oh shit, man, Footty is trippin,' this bitch is pregnant. So, he snatched his gun out of the window and ran back to the car.

"Yo, what happened, son?"

"Footty, man you are not right, why didn't you tell me that girl was pregnant?"

"Who pregnant?"

"The girl in the house."

"No, she is not."

"Yes, she is, look at the size of her stomach." Day Day turned his head and pointed at Sheema. When he turned back and looked at Footty, Footty had a nickel-plated-forty-five Magnum pointed right at his face.

"Yo Footty, what the hell, man, stop playing."

"Do it look like the fuck I am playing, now go over there and shoot both of them, or I am going to shoot your ass."

"Footty, what is going on with you, is everything okay?"

"Man, fuck that, what are you going to do, Day Day?"

"Footty, I'm not shooting no pregnant girl, you're just going to have to shoot me."

Footty lowered his gun, and said, "You didn't really think I would shoot you, now, did you?"

"No, but you be playing a little too much."

Footty said, "Oh shit, here they come."

Day Day turned to look, then Footty pulled the trigger. Day Day's brains splattered all over the passenger side window and door. Then Footty shot him again, just to be sure. Ra Ra and Sheema heard the shots and ran to the door to see what was going on. She saw someone get out of the car acting like they were hurt. She ran over to him too asked if he was okay, until she saw the mask on his face and a gun in his hand. She turned around and ran back towards the house. Then Footty raised his gun and fired three shots in her direction. *Block ah, block ah, block ah* Ra Ra was screaming, telling Sheema to get down. Then he let off a few shots of his own. Sheema did a swan dive to the ground, as Footty and Ra Ra shot it out until they were empty. Footty then ran off. Ra Ra ran over to help Sheema up, but she wouldn't move. He kept calling her name, so he grabbed her and picked her up. Blood was everywhere. Sheema caught all three bullets in her back. Ra Ra called 9-1-1 and told them that his girlfriend had been shot. With sheema in his arms, Ra Ra took off running towards any hospital. That may have been miles away, but he didn't care. Sheema was dying, and he needed to save her life.

The doctors moved Rudy Ray from the intensive care unit to the recovery room. He came out of his coma and was no longer on life support. Deena was so happy that she had Rudy back. The doctors were still baffled that Rudy Ray was awake. They asked Deena did she do or say anything to Rudy that might have helped. Deena said, "No, I just came from using the bathroom, and his eyes were open. While all along saying to herself, "If I knew playing with this nigga dick would have woken him, I would have done it a long time ago." As she giggled, Deena walked over and kissed Rudy Ray on his forehead and asked him how he was feeling this morning. Rudy opened his eyes, then closed them back, quickly falling asleep. He would do that for the next few days, until all the medication wore off in his system.

Sheema was in surgery for over nine hours. The doctors did everything they could do to save her life. All three bullets went straight through her body and missed all her major organs. She will pull through and live, but the twins didn't make it. Sitting in the waiting room were Carmen, Mya, Chippy, Pooh Bear, and Ra Ra. The doctors came in and gave everybody the good news and the bad news. Ra Ra just sat there staring into space with blood all over him. All the girls began to cry, and Pooh Bear was trying to talk to Ra Ra, but Ra Ra didn't respond. See Sheema never knew who her dad was, and her mom died when she was a baby. She had a foster mother that didn't give a shit about her. All she cared about was that monthly check that she was getting. So, Carmen, Mya, and Chippy were the only family she knew. Ra Ra got up and walked out of the hospital, not saying a word. Pooh Bear had a bad feeling about him leaving but let him go anyway to give him some time to himself. Pooh Bear asked the doctor could they go in and see Sheema. The doctor said, "Well, she is in the ICU, so I can only give you a few minutes, she needs a lot of rest." Ra Ra walked all the way home. In front of his house were four police cars, and the car that Day Day had gotten killed in that was all taped off. Ra Ra opened his front door, then a car pulled up with two detectives in it. They had been following him ever since he left the hospital. They got out and walked in right behind him. "Excuse me, Mister Raheem, you need to come with us down to homicide so that we could ask you a few questions." Ra Ra sat in an interrogation room for hours, as they watched him from behind the two-way mirror. He was tired, and hungry, and wasn't talking. The only thing he told them was somebody shot his girlfriend and ran off, and he didn't know who it was. About a half an hour later, a female officer came in and brought Ra Ra a sandwich and a soda. "Raheem, you would really be helping yourself if you tell us what happened. Here is a pen and piece of paper, give us a statement and you are free to go home." Ra Ra ate the sandwich and drank the soda, letting out a big old belch, then told the cops to get lost. The other cop ran into the room, gripped Ra Ra up, and yelled in his face, "Who killed that guy in the car, was it you, you little punk, who, was it?"

"Man, get your hands the fuck off of me and find out who shot my baby mom, that's what you need to be doing, and leave me the hell alone!"

Both cops left the interrogation room to talk. "Look partner, you know in forty-eight hours we are going to have to let him go, I don't think he did it, look at his face, he seems to be lost, like something is missing, his eyes are filled with nothing but pain. I say we let him go."

"Okay, we can let him go after we fingerprint him, and if one, I mean

106

one of his fingerprints show up on that car, I'm going to book him for murder.

Footty woke up laying on the floor of an abandoned house. His wet high was wearing off, and he didn't know how he got there. He stood up and stumbled into the bathroom to take a leak. He tried to turn on the lights, but they didn't turn on. He was like what the fuck and tried it again. "I know these mother fuckers didn't turn my electric off." Then Footty looked around. "Hold up, where the fuck am I?" Footty ran back into the room from which he came. His mask and his forty-five were laying on the floor. Footty picked up his gun; it was empty. "Why is my gun empty, and who fucken mask is this? Shit, I got blood all over me, what the fuck did I do?" Footty left and made his way home. He then jumped in his shower and changed his clothes, grabbed a bag of dope out of his top dresser drawer, and started snorting. Three snorts into his bag, his phone rang. "Hello, who is this?"

"It's me, dog, where are you?"

"I'm home, why what's up?"

"Have you seen Day Day?"

"No, not since the day I saw yall together, is everything good?"

"I don't know, I haven't seen him all day, the last I heard he was supposed to be doing his laundry at the Circle K."

"Oh, did you hear somebody got their wig split out at Tasker?"

"Any word on who it was?"

"No, but if I hear something, I will keep you posted."

"Alright, you do that, and when I see Day Day I will tell him to call you." Footty hung up and got back to snorting his dope. "Man fuck Day Day, I don't like his bitch ass no more anyway, and as soon as I see him, I might smack the shit out of him."

CHAPTER 13

Visiting hours were over and even though they only had a few minutes to see Sheema, they felt a lot better, knowing she was alive and being able to touch her. Pooh Bear drove the girl's home; he dropped Chippy off first, then Carmen and Mya. He really didn't have anything to say to either one of them, but now wasn't the time. Carmen and Mya were visibly upset, and Carmen was taking it the hardest. Pooh Bear pulled up and walked Carmen to the door, and Mya followed behind them. Carmen let herself in and begged Pooh Bear not to leave her alone. She asked if she could please talk to him. Pooh Bear didn't want to, but he agreed, and they all went in. Carmen sat next to him and started explaining herself. Pooh Bear just listened while mean mugging the shit out of Mya. Mya came over and stood over top of Carmen and Pooh Bear. She started to speak, but Pooh Bear wasn't trying to hear it. Mya leaned over and told Pooh Bear to look at her. Pooh Bear went to say something, buy Mya kissed him right in the mouth. Pooh Bear went to push her away, but Carmen told him not to, that it was okay. "Pooh Bear, I know you mad at me and Mya, so we want to make it up to you." Mya kissed Pooh Bear again, but this time he didn't push her away. Carmen got up and started taking off all her clothes, then joined right in. It would be a night Pooh Bear would never forget.

Finally, all the medication had run through Rudy Ray's system, and he was now sitting up talking to Deena. BlackJack walked into his hospital room and Rudy Ray's face lit up. "What's up, my nigga, how are you feeling, it's good to see you awake?"

Deena said, "Amen to that! Rudy I am going to get me something to eat so you and Jack can talk." Deena left the room.

Jack gave Rudy Ray a big hug. "Yo, you had me nervous for a minute, I thought you wasn't going to make it."

Rudy Ray laughed. "Come on Jack, it's going to take a lot more than that to kill an old hound dog like me."

"I know that's right." Jack replied, "but on the more serious note, how is your leg right now?"

"Not so good, but the doctors said with some hard work and rehabilitation I should walk again, maybe with a slight limp."

"Rudy Ray, I need to ask you something, do you know who put that hit out on you?"

"No, I don't, but the guy who shot me look very familiar, I just can't place where I've seen him before." Rudy Ray's mind was racing.

"Well just so you know, I took care of that for you?"

"You took care of what, Jack?"

"Both of them son of a bitches, as we speak, they are both taking dirt naps."

"Good looken, Jack, how did you find out who they were because I never saw who was driving that Yukon? The windows were all tented out."

"You remember Duck from the two four?"

"Yes."

"Well money talk and bullshit walk."

Rudy Ray sat there quiet for a minute, then said, "Jack, think about it, I don't even know who the driver was, so how do he?"

Jack thought about that shit for a minute. Rudy Ray had a point, Duck must know more than he had led Jack to believe. Now come to think of it, why was it so easy for him to get Kato? Duck has some explaining to do. Jack pulled out ten grand and gave it to Rudy Ray. "This should hold you and Deena until you get back on your feet."

"Thank you, Jack, you are a true friend." Rudy Ray took the money, and shook Jack's hand, then Jack left.

The next day, E-money was banging on Footty's front door. Footty ran to the door half asleep. He peeked out his window and saw a car parked in the middle of the street, running with the driver's-side door open. *knock knock knock* E-money banged on the door again.

Footty yelled out, "Who the fuck is banging on my door like that?"

"It's me, open up."

Footty opened the door. "What's up, man, are you alright?"

"Fuck no, I'm not alright. You know that guy I was telling you about, that got his head cracked the fuck open out in Tasker?"

"Yes, I remember you telling me about it."

"Well fuck man, it was Day Day."

"You are joking, right?"

"No, and the word on the street is that fucking bitch-ass Ra Ra did it in front of his own house."

"Whose house?"

"Ra Ra's house."

"What the hell was Day Day doing over there by himself?"

"I don't know, but this shit doesn't sound right, I think they set him up."

Footty said, "Let me get dressed, we can move on them niggas right now." E-money and Footty got in the car and pulled off.

Footty and E-money circled around the whole entire Tasker projects looking for Ra Ra. As E-money drove past Ra Ra's house, Footty kept having flashbacks. "What the hell is wrong with me?" Footty was thinking. Ra Ra was nowhere to be found. The car they were driving needed some gas, so E-money stopped at the ATM machine on Twenty-Third and Snyder Avenue to get some money. The gas station he needed to go to was on Twenty-Fourth and Passyunk. As they drove past the Save-A-Lot store, Footty spotted Pooh Bear helping his mom put groceries in the trunk of their car. E-money slowed the car down. Mom Parker noticed them out of the corner of her eye. E-money turned the car up into the parking lot. Mom Parker was still smiling like she didn't know what time it was. Both Footty and E-money's eyes were fixed on Pooh Bear. Mom Parker took her pocketbook off her shoulder and sat it down in the trunk. She opened it and took out a 9 mm handgun, then she said, "Pooh Bear, I need you to listen to mama, okay? At the count of three, I need you to take off running, one, two, three." Pooh Bear took off and E-money went after him, but mom Parker spun from behind her car and let loose on them. *block ah, block ah, block block, block ah, block ah* Footty said, "What the fuck?" He tried to shoot back, but mom Parker let off two more, *block ah, block ah*, both hitting Footty dead in the center of his chest. Footty head snapped back as he let out a loud scream. She let loose a few more. *block ah, block ah, block ah* Footty was yelling at E-money, telling him to get the fuck out of there. E- money spent off. Mom Parker jumped into her car and left. She called Jack to let him know what had just gone down. BlackJack stopped what he was doing and went to Save-A-Lot. He walked in and asked the guard could he speak to the manager. The guard pointed to the manager's door. As he walked outside to talk to the police, Jack knocked on the manager's door and walked in. "Excuse me, sir, but you can't come in here."

The manager looked up and said, "Jack, is that you?"

"Yes, it's me."

"Then you must be here for this."

The manager handed Jack the videotape from the camera overlooking the parking lot. Jack put the tape underneath his shirt, then he pulled out a knot full of money. The manager told Jack that wouldn't be necessary. "I could never repay you for what you done for me." See when Jack was just a teenager, he killed two men trying to abduct the manager's daughters. Jack put his money away and left the store. Jack got to the house and destroyed to tape. Mom Parker was glad to see it done, she knew with no evidence, she would be in the clear. She just needed to fall back.

E-money pulled over in Jerry's Corner's parking lot. Footty fell out of the car, down to his knees, and started throwing up all over the place. E-money helped him pull off his shirt and then pulled Footty's bulletproof vest over his head. Footty rolled over onto his back and laid on the ground. He had two-big-red spots on the front of his chest. Luckily, he had that vest on or he would be dead right now. Footty gathered himself and caught his breath. He picked his shirt up and got back in the car. "Are you alright now?"

"No, I'm not alright, that bitch just tried to kill me, who was she?"

"I don't know, maybe it was his mom or something."

"His mom, naw, it couldn't be, her ass was too fat."

"Well shit, maybe it was his sister, then, it doesn't matter, if I ever see her again, I will put two in her chest, and we will see how the bitch like that." Footty must have just wanted to hear himself talk. He might have done just what he said, but he had no idea the wrath that would come behind him shooting mom Parker.

Six days later, everybody was at Day Day's mom's house. They had just got back from the cemetery, burying Day Day. All his family was there and so was Footty, and E-money. Day Day' mom had a big dinner in the memory of her son. As she fixed Footty a plate, he gave her a hug and a kiss, and told her how much he was going to miss his friend. She hugged him back and told him to be strong and Day Day had always looked up to him, and not to worry, because the police would find out who killed him. Footty took his plate, then went into the living room where they were showing some home movies of Day Day from when he was a little boy. E-money couldn't stop thinking about what happened to his man. He kept saying to himself, "Why would Day Day ride over to Tasker by himself, it didn't make sense, there is something I'm missing, I just can't put my finger on it." Footty came over and sat down next to E-money and started to eat his food.

E-money looked at him and said, "How can you eat at a time like this?"

"It's easy, you use this thing called a fork."

E-money jumped up and went to walk away. Footty grabbed his arm and said, "Yo E, I'm just joking man, why are you so uptight, I am just as upset as you are that our hommie is gone, that doesn't mean we are not supposed to eat."

E-money sat back down, and said, "You know what, Footty, you are right." So, he picked up his glass and gave Day Day a big toast.

As everyone joined in, Footty started getting dizzy. He had two quick flashbacks. "What the hell?" he said.

E-money looked down on him. "Yo Footty, is you ok?"

Footty said, "Naw man, I think I had too much to drink." Two more flashbacks hit him. "Please E-money, I need you to take me home." E-money dropped Footty off at his house. Footty walked in his door and passed out on the couch. He stayed there until the next day.

Pooh Bear stopped by Ra Ra's house to check on his buddy. He had not seen or heard from him ever since that day at the hospital. Pooh Bear knocked and knocked, but there was no answer. So, he peeked into the front window to see if anybody was home. The lights were out, and the house looked deserted. Pooh Bear got back in the car and drove off. About six blocks away, Pooh Bear saw Ra Ra walking down the street looking a mess. He was dirty and smelled bad. Ra Ra turned and looked at Pooh Bear, then kept walking. Pooh Bear rolled up on the side of him and told him to get in the car. Ra Ra just paid him no mind. "Where the hell was, he going?" Pooh Bear thought. See Ra Ra had lost his mind. Losing his twins must have been the straw that broke the camel's back. Pooh Bear pulled over and got out. The closer and closer he got to Ra Ra; the worse Ra Ra looked. His hair looked like it hadn't been brushed in weeks. His teeth were yellow, his hands were dirty, and he smelled like a bag of shit. Pooh Bear knew his hommie was gone, but he needed to save him anyway.

Over at big Buddha's house, with Leak and Joe Hot dead, and Ra Ra not all there, Pooh Bear decided to hang out down Twenty-Second and Manton Street. When he arrived, there was a big poker game going on, and of course, niggas were playing Madden. Bets were everywhere. Pooh Bear pulled up a chair to the poker table. He said to himself, "I'm going to get some of this money, first, then I'm going over there and take all that Madden money." Niggas at the table started laughing. See the cats at the poker table were glad Pooh Bear was there. They knew he brought a lot of money with him, but the suckers playing Madden were shook. They knew it was only a matter of time before Pooh Bear took all their money. All the guys that hung out at Buddha's house were cool. Pooh Bear felt safe for a change. He put all his troubles behind him and was enjoying his day. So, he called up The Bottom of the Sea and ordered a dungeness crab platter with extra old bay seasoning. Pooh Bear continued to play poker until his food arrived. He paid the delivery guy, then sat down to eat. He was up like six hundred dollars, so he felt like playing some Madden when he finished eating. He picked up the PlayStation 3 controller and was ready for some work. The poker game stopped, and all bets were on the football game. Pooh Bear wasted no time. His first opponent lost twenty-one nothing; that sucker had to pay double. The next game was forty-nine to fourteen, it was too easy, and Pooh Bear was loven it.

Footty woke up and went into the kitchen. He opened the freezer and grabbed a bottle of wet. He then went back into the living room and dipped one of the cigarettes into the small bottle and lit it up. When he finished smoking it, he was high as shit, but he wanted more, so he lit up the other one. Halfway through the cigarette, he heard somebody calling his name. "Shit, who the fuck is that?" as he took a few more puffs. Then he heard it again, so he went to the steps and called out, "Who is that, what do you want, how did you get in my house?" Footty pulled out his gun and ran up the steps. He heard somebody calling his name again. "Yo, who the fuck is that? I'm telling you right now, I will shoot." The sound was coming from Footty's bedroom all the way at the other end of the hall. Footty crept down the hallway with his guns drawn. He felt like he was walking on air. It seems like the hallway would never end. The closer he got to his room door, the louder the voice got. He finally got to his bedroom, took a deep breath, then kicked the door open. As the door fell off the hinges, all he could see was darkness and sitting on the end of his bed was Day Day. He had a big hole in the back of his head and his eyes were all black. Footty closed his eyes then opened them back up. Day Day was still sitting there. Footty yelled out, "What do you want, why are you here, what do you want to know?" Day Day just kept saying, "Why did you kill me, Footty, I always looked up to you?" At that point it all came back to him. Footty fell to his knees in tears and told Day Day he was so sorry. He said he didn't mean to do it and continued to cry until he passed out on the floor. He lay there for the next few days.

CHAPTER 14

P ooh Bear showed big Buddha some love as he was about to leave. "Yo Buddha, I am out."

"Alright Pooh Bear, when is the next time I am going to see you?"

"I can't call it, you know a brother be busy, you fill me?"

"Yes, I can dig it, I'll see you when I see you then."

Pooh Bear left out of the door and got in his car. He won like two thousand dollars, so he felt like having some fun. "Fuck it, I feel like going to the strip club and hanging out with some whores." So, he shot up to North Philly to Twenty-Second and Indiana to a spot called The Down Low. It was in the cut and the whores were cheap. Pooh Bear parked his car and walked up the steps to the strip club, paid ten dollars to get in, then gave the bouncer another hundred not to check him for weapons. The bouncer opened the door and bitches were everywhere. The music was pumpin.' Frank Ocean's song was playing: "What's a man to a mob, what's a mob to a king, what's a king to a God, what's a god to a non-believer, who don't, believe in anything." The club was poppin.' The bitches were walking around butt naked and ready to suck some dick. Two dancers walked up to Pooh Bear and asked him did he want a lap dance. Both of

117

those bitches were talking at the same time. He was like "Hold up, both of yall sound just a like."

"Of course, we do, we are twins."

Pooh Bear's dick got hard. "Alright then, I got one question to ask y'all before we do all this lap dancing shit."

"And what's that, cutie pie?"

"Is any one of y'all bitches fucking?" The girls laughed.

"Nigga, you are in North Philadelphia, all we do is fuck."

That's all Pooh Bear needed to hear. The bitches started to dance, and shake, and pop their asses all over Pooh Bear and he was loven it. One was giving him a lap dance while the other was dropping it and locking it. I mean this bitch ass was snapping like a slinky. She had a tattoo of a man on her ass, and she made him walk from one ass cheek to the other. Pooh Bear was like "What the fuck did she just do?" Then Pooh Bear sat up as she put her pussy right in his face. All he could smell was a sweet aroma that was coming from between her legs. It was driving him crazy. The DJ was playing all the latest jams and niggas were spending money. It was wall-to-wall ass up in the house. And for every two dicks, there were ten whores. Bitches were dancing on the bar, swinging on the poles, and selling pussy. Pooh Bear started sucking on both of their titties at the same time, one nipple after another, as he slipped dollar bills into both of their G-strings. Then of course, a fight broke out. Now it was time to go. Pooh Bear got up and left. As he walked down the street to his car, he could hear high-heeled shoes hitting the pavement behind him. Pooh Bear turned around; it was the twins.

"Where are y'all going?"

"I thought we were going with you."

"Shit, I'm about to go home."

"Look mister, after all that, we want some dick. Now are you going to fuck us or what?"

Both talking at the same damn time. Pooh Bear looked at both, and in the light, they were even better looking. "Okay, fuck it," he said, "y'all get in." Twenty minutes later, they all pulled up to the Blue Moon Motel, on Fifty-Second and Westminster, in the heart of West Philadelphia. Pooh Bear paid for the room and asked the cashier for twelve magnums. They all got onto the elevator and got off on the third floor. Pooh Bear unlocked the room door, and they went in. He told the girls to get undressed, and that he had to use the bathroom quick. As he was taking a leak, Pooh Bear counted his money and checked his gun. "These bitches will never catch me slippin'." Pooh Bear walked out of the bathroom and both girls were laying naked on the bed. They both had nice shapes. One twin was completely shaved, and the other one had a nice little trimmed bush. Pooh Bear thought "Wow, I got the best of both worlds, which one of these bad bitches, do I want to fuck first?" He couldn't make up his mind, so he said, "Fuck it, I will flip a coin, heads, bald, tails, bush." Pooh Bear flipped his coin and it landed on tails. So, he told the one with the hairy-ass pussy to open her legs so he could fuck her.

The girls said, "Wait, before you fuck us, you have to pay us."

Pooh Bear was like "Oh my bad, here you go, I almost forgot," then gave them their money.

Now it was time to put in some work. Pooh Bear took his clothes off, climbed up between her legs, put her legs high in the air, then stuck his dick inside of her. The pussy was hot and sticky. Pooh Bear started banging the shit out of her. She closed her eyes and started moaning. He fucked her pussy for about ten minutes then switched to her sister. Her sister's pussy was even wetter and a little bit tighter. Pooh Bear was tearing that pussy up, missionary style. He was hammering the shit out of her, but she kept telling him to go harder. Then he switched back to the other sister. This went on for the next two hours, every ten minutes he would go back and forth. He would put his dick in one of them and be French kissing the other one at the same time. He told both to get up on their knees. There were two-round-plump asses in his face, and they were the same size, with fat pussy lips sticking out from the back. Pooh Bear started popping both, five strokes here, five strokes there, until he pulled his dick out, took off his rubber, and came all over both. He would continue to fuck these twin bitches for the rest of the night. He had to admit, both of those bitches were whores, but they had some real good pussy.

It was getting close to the time for Bay Boy to come home. He had been calling Ra Ra for the last week and was getting no answer. Worry began to set in. He didn't know what was going on. He heard what happened to Day Day, Sheema, and the twins through the grapevine, but did not have any details. Then he went back to his dorm room and started writing Pooh Bear a kite. When he was done writing, he sealed it in an envelope, put a stamp on it, and sent it out right away. Three days later, mom Parker pulled up and parked in front of her house, when she noticed the mailman had come by. "Man, these bill collectors don't play." As she was going through the mail, she saw a letter to Pooh Bear. She went to the steps and called his name to see if he was home. Pooh Bear hollered back letting her know he was upstairs. "Boy, you got a letter down here from Bay Boy." Pooh Bear went down the steps, got the letter, and went back to his room so he could read it." He opened it up, and it said,

"To Pooh Bear, what is it looking like out there? I hope you know I will be home in a couple of weeks. I heard what happened to Sheema, but where is Ra Ra? I have been calling him for the past week. Did he move without letting me know? The word on the street is that he rocked Day Day. I would have tried to call you sooner, but I had to take you off my call list for a minute. Please tell me you have seen him, it's not like him not to answer his phone. I hope you still have that present for me when I touch the streets because Footty and E-money got some explaining to do. Oh, and just so you know, I got my GED while I was in here, I couldn't be happier. I am finally done with school; college never was for me. Pooh Bear, I need you to listen, I know you are at war out there, but I need you to do me a favor. I need you to fall back and wait until I get home, then me, you, and Ra Ra will put an end to this bullshit."

Pooh Bear felt bad, so much stuff had been going on that he forgot all about keeping Bay Boy in the loop. As a matter of fact, he hadn't been to see him either. What was he to do, should he write him, or tell him over the phone, or should he let him come home and see it for himself?

"Hey girls, what's going on?" Sheema started to smile as Carmen, Mya, and Chippy came into her hospital room.

"Please tell me yall got some real food in one of those bags because I can't eat not one more bite of this hospital slop." Chippy pulled out a cheesesteak and started to tease Sheema with it. All the girls started laughing as Sheema almost fell out of the bed trying to grab that cheesesteak out of Chippy's hand. "Stop playing yall, please give it to me." Chippy gave Sheema the cheesesteak, and in less than two minutes, it was gone. "Damn Chippy, where the fuck did you get that cheesesteak from, that mother fucker was good? I need another one."

"No, greedy ass, we don't even know if we are supposed to be feeding you."

"So how have you been feeling?" Carmen asked.

"I'm a lot better, my back be hurting sometimes, but other than that, I'm good."

Mya yelled out, "Bitch, ain't nothing wrong with you, when are you getting the hell out of here, this place is depressing?"

"I don't know, hopefully in the next few days. If it wasn't for Ra Ra, I would be dead right now, where is he at, anyway?" All the girls stopped laughing and everything went quiet. "Well, have anybody seen him?"

Chippy cleared her throat, then spoke up, and said, "Sheema, Ra Ra is not doing so good."

"What do you mean?"

"See, ever since you lost the twins, Ra Ra has not been the same. The last time I saw him, he acted like he didn't even know me, he was dirty, and was sleeping on the streets." Sheema started to cry. "Plus, there is a rumor out that he is the one who killed that boy, Day Day, from Wilson." Just then, some detectives knocked on her room door and kindly let themselves in.

"If you ladies can please excuse yourselves, we need a few minutes to ask Sheema some questions." The girls left out of the room right away, then the detectives introduced themselves.

"Hi, Sheema, I am Detective Mickey Turner, and this is my partner, Homicide Detective Cindy Watson."

"Okay, so what do you want with me?"

"We just want to know what happened that night, who shot you, and why did Raheem kill Day Day?"

"Ra Ra didn't kill anybody."

"How do you know?"

"Because I was there."

"Well, somebody killed Day Day, was it you?"

That shit made Sheema mad. "You know what, fuck you, and your partner, I'm not saying another word."

"I am sorry, Sheema, I didn't mean to offend you, I am just trying to solve a homicide, so please, can you tell us how it all went down?"

Sheema really didn't want to talk to these pigs, but she could clearly see they were trying to pin this homicide on Ra Ra. So, she began to speak, "Me and Ra Ra was standing in the living room, talking about what we were going to do about our twins that I was about the have, when we heard a loud boom outside."

"A loud boom like what, a car crash, or a loud boom like a gunshot?"

"It was like a gunshot, so we went to the door, to see what it was, when we see a man get out of the car. He looked like he was injured, so I went to help, then I noticed he had a mask on, and a gun in his hand."

"Okay, did you see anybody else in the car?"

"No, but I didn't have time to look, once I saw the gun, I turned around to run, and that's when he shot me."

"And where was Ra Ra when all this was happening?"

"He was standing in the door, telling me not to go over there, but I went over there, anyway, then I heard him yelling, telling me to get down, that's when everything went black, that's all I can remember."

The two detectives stood up and stepped to the side, as they both were waying there options, "I don't know about you, but her story sounds credible, so…"

"You believe her, because I don't?"

"Alright partner, think about it, the medical examiner said that the victim had to have been shot at close range, which means, the shooter had to have been in the car." The two detectives turned back to Sheema and said, "That will be all, if we have any more questions, we will be in touch." Then the detectives gave Sheema their business cards, telling her, if she remembers anything else, to please give them a call.

After washing his face in the sink, Footty reached up and grabbed a towel to dry his face off. He stood there, looking at himself in the mirror. He had just taken four Percocets to stop his head from hurting. "Damn, what the fuck, how long have I been out? Footty, you need to get yourself together man, I don't know how them niggas pop pills like that every day, I can't do it, and that fucken wet, that shit is for the birds, I'll stick to snorting my dope." he then went back into his room to get his daily fix. He could see that the door was knocked off the hinges and he was wondering what happened, until he had another flashback. He grabbed the side of his head and started shaking it back and forth. "How could I do such a thing to Day Day?" The guilt was consuming him as he felt so empty inside. Flashes of Day Day's face kept going through his mind. As he walked back into the bathroom, he started staring back at himself in the mirror. "Footty, what have you done?" As tears started flowing from his eyes, he banged his fist up and down on the sink, begging Day Day to forgive him for what he had done. He started throwing shit all over the bathroom, screaming, "No, no, no, I didn't mean to do it." He then pulled his gun from his waist and put it into his mouth. Still staring in the mirror, he cocked the hammer back and began to apply pressure on to the trigger.

Just as he blew his brains out, in his mind, before he did it, his cell phone rang, and it was E-money.

Rudy Ray's physical therapy was going well. He was way ahead of schedule, so far ahead, that the doctors said he was well enough to go home. Deena was happy. After all this time, she could finally get her some dick and have somebody to sleep next to. The doctors gave Rudy Ray his discharge papers, then told him he had to come back at least three times a week for therapy. Deena took all the paperwork and neatly tucked it away in her bag. Then she helped Rudy Ray get dressed so that they could leave. Rudy Ray called Jack and told him he was being released. Jack liked the sound of that, his man was about to come home. Jack told Rudy Ray to give him about thirty minutes, and he would come up to the hospital and pick him and Deena up.

Footty took the gun out of his mouth and watched his cell phone light up. As it kept ringing, he put his gun on the back of the toilet so that he could throw some warm water on his face. He sat down on the side of the tub thinking about whether he should tell somebody what he had done. So, after about fifteen minutes of convincing himself, he decided to spill the beans to E-money, thinking he would know exactly what to do. Footty picked up his phone and returned E-money's missed call. E-money's phone started ringing. *ring ring, ring ring* "Hello." Footty didn't say anything. "Hello, is anybody there?" E-money looked down at the number on his phone to see who was calling him. "Footty, is this you?"

"Yes, it's me."

"Well why didn't you say anything, I was about to hang up on you?"

"My bad player."

"Footty, I was just calling you a few minutes ago, are you alright?"

"Yes, I'm good."

"That's what's up, I haven't heard from you in a couple of days, I thought I would give you a call, to check on you."

"Good looken."

"Well anyway, what can I do for you? I know you was calling me for a reason."

"Yes, I was, I need to tell you something."

"Alright, I'm all ears."

"E-money, I know who killed Day Day."

E-money got quiet. "Who?" he said. As Footty was about to tell him it was him that did it, E-money snapped the fuck out. "Who was it, Footty, tell me who it was, and I will kill their whole fucken family, I don't give a fuck who it is, just give me a name, and they are as good as dead?"

So Footty thought about it real hard, and then said, "It was Ra Ra and Pooh Bear that set him up."

E-money was hot, breathing heavy in the phone. "Alright Footty, say no more, I got something for both of those cowards."

CHAPTER 15

I t was about eight thirty in the morning. Jack was taking out the trash, throwing it into the dumpster. As he walked back in the house, there were some detectives parked in a white car, watching him. They radioed into dispatch telling them that they had a positive ID on the location of their suspect. Backup shortly arrived, then both detectives got out, and walked over to Jack's house, banging on the door. *boom boom boom* Within a few seconds, mom Parker was asking "Who is it?"

"It's the police, now open up."

Mom Parker's heart dropped into her stomach. She thought they were there for her so she took a deep breath, then opened the door and said, "Can I help you?"

"Sorry to bother you ma'am, but is Jack Parker here, please don't lie, we just saw him walk into this house?"Jack came downstairs and told Tina to move out of the way, and that he would handle it from here, "Sir, are you Jack Parker?"

"Yes, I am, why, what's up?"

"I will tell you what's up, we have a warrant for your arrest, for the murders of three white males at a supermarket in the suburbs."

Jack said, "No, you must be mistaken, I don't know what the fuck you are talking about."

"Sir, please turn around and put your hands behind your back." Mom Parker started to cry. "Jack Parker, you have the right to remain silent, anything you say, or do, will be held against you in the court of law, you have the right to an attorney, if you cannot afford one, one will be appointed to you…" Jack was in some deep shit. He told Tina to stop crying and to wait for his phone call. The police took Jack out the house and put him in the back of a paddy wagon and drove him away.

Pooh Bear went straight home after his mom called and told him what had happened. He spent the night at Carmen's house like he had been doing for the last three days. "Mom, what did they lock my dad up for?"

"Three counts of murder?"

"Are you kidding me? My dad didn't kill anyone."

"Of course, he didn't, it must be a mistake." Tina picked up the phone and called Rudy Ray and Deena to tell them that Jack got arrested. Rudy asked how much his bail was. Mom Parker told him she didn't know, because he hadn't called her yet with any information. Rudy Ray said, "Okay, but as soon as you hear something, call me back." Sixteen hours later, Jack called, telling Tina he was at the round house, and the judge did not give him bail. He said that he was being charged with three counts of first-degree murder. Tina's worst nightmares were coming true. Jack told her that he would be on the next bus headed to the Curran Fromhold Correctional Facilitty, or CFCF, and he would call her with further instructions. He then asked her to put Pooh Bear on the phone.

"Yo, what's up, Pop?"

"Look here son, your dad is caught up in some deep shit and I am going to be away for a while, you are now the man of the house, and you will always protect your mother. You oversee all my businesses and all my stashes. You are never to use Norm and Norma, under any circumstances, do you understand me?"

"Yes sir."

"Okay, now give your mother back the phone. Tina, listen to me, honey, we are going to get through this so don't worry."

"Jack, I already know that I have never doubted you, and I am not about to start now."

"That's my girl."

"I love you, Jack."

"I love you, too, Tina." Then Jack blew his wife a kiss, and he hung the phone up.

Ring ring, ring ring, ring ring, "Hello."

"Ah, yes, can I please speak to a Mister Sun?"

"Speaking, how can I help you?"

"Well, this is the crime tip line calling to let you know that tip you called in led to the arrest of the suspect that was sought after in the supermarket murders, and you qualify for the ten thousand dollar reward. All you need to do to collect it is to bring your ID with you when you come to get it."

"Thanks, but no thanks, I won't be collecting it, I just wanted to be a good Samaritan and help our law enforcement officers get at least one bad guy off of the street."

Are you sure about that, sir? If that is the case, would you like to donate it to charity?"

"I don't care who you give it to, I'm just not collecting it."

"Alright then, we have quite a few to choose from."

"It doesn't matter, just choose anyone."

"Sir, I can't do that for you, it's against our policy. You must choose one for yourself."

"Okay, donate it to the Make-A-Wish Foundation, and make the donor's name anonymous."

"Nice choice, Make-A-Wish Foundation it is, thank you for your time, Mister Sun. Bye-bye now."

OG Sun hung the phone up, laughing his ass off, saying, "I finally got this son of a dog's ass. Who said it doesn't pay to be a mother fucken rat?

As the prison bus pulled into the back of CFCF, Jack wondered how the fuck they knew it was him who killed those men in the supermarket. Somebody was snitching, but who? The prison bus doors opened, and the sheriffs told all the prisoners to get off the bus hand cuffed in sets of two. To Jack, that shit was really corny. As each inmate walked through the sliding doors, the Correctional Officers, or CO, told them to stand against the walls. There was another CO sitting at a desk with four crates filled with cold packs and milk. Then another sliding door opened, and the CO told everybody to "listen up, I need y'all to follow me and go into that holding cell, as you pass that desk with the four crates, grab yourself a cold pack." After everybody was in a holding cell, another door opened from the other side. The CO then took everybody into the notorious receiving room. After that, he jammed each one of them into an even smaller holding cell. There were at least ten cells full of people ahead of the cell that Jack was in, and they were filled to the limit. Jack shook his head; he knew he was going to be in that receiving room for at least a couple of days. See the receiving room in CFCF was one rough stop. They moved you from cell to cell every six to eight hours until you get to cell number one. Well, Jack was in cell number twelve, which meant he had a lot of time to think about how he was going to get out of this one. After about a day and a half, the CO finally called Jack's name. He knew the routine. It was time for him to get his picture taken for his armband and fill out his phone-list paper. The CO snapped Jack's picture, then Jack handed her his phone list. The CO told Jack that he could get up to five different numbers on his list, but he only had one. Jack said one number was all he needed as he stepped to the side so he could get his one phone call. He picked up the payphone and dialed his home number. His phone started ringing. "Hello."

"Hey baby."

"Hi honey, what's up, where do they have you now?"

"I am at c f c f in the receiving room."

"Jack, please tell me I can come and see you?"

"No, not yet, I haven't even got out of quarantine yet."

"And how long is that going to take?"

"I don't know, don't get me to lying, maybe like two to four weeks."

"That long?"

"Yes, unfortunately, that's how the system works."

"How are you feeling?"

"Jack, you know I'm worried to death."

"Don't be, you know, and I know, I didn't kill anybody."

"Did you eat anything?"

"No, they only gave out cold packs, and I don't know where that so-called meat came from." The CO yelled over to Jack, telling him his time was over.

"Jack, please be careful."

"I got you babe, no need for you to worry, I got this."

"Do you need me to do anything for you?"

"Yes, get me J P Walker."

"I am, already on it. Anything else?"

"No."

"I love you, Jack."

"I love you too, princess." Jack dropped the phone and went back to his holding cell.

Twelve more hours went by, and Jack was still in the receiving room. Niggas were sleep everywhere, on the floor, on top of each other, underneath the benches, on the toilet, anywhere a nigga could fit, he was there sleeping. It smelled like piss, underarms, ass, and feet. If it was funky, it was in his cell. Finally, Jack was called to take a shower. They gave him a towel, a washcloth, a blanket, a bag of personal stuff, and a fucken carrot suit. The CO told Jack to take a shower and change into that orange jumper. After Jack finished taking his shower, he was told to go into a different holding cell and take a cup with him so he could submit a piss specimen, then the nurse would be seeing him shortly. The nurse called Jack back into her office. He sat down, and a nurse began to ask him a series of questions. She gave him a needle so she could check him for tuberculosis; she swabbed his cheeks, to make sure he wasn't HIV positive; she checked his weight. Jack was tired and hungry. It would be two more hours before it was any more movement. The CO then called twenty-five people, with Jack being one of them. The CO then moved all the new recruits to another holding cell, then he hit the button and told the bubble he was ready for movement. The bubble opened the door, and everybody walked across the small hallway into section B 1 1. The CO made everybody line up against the wall. He then told them to put their blankets down on the floor. Then he said to listen very closely to what he had to say because he was going to only say it once. "I need you to take off your socks and your shoes and sit them down in front of you. Then turn your ass around and put your hands up on the wall; spread your fucken legs; don't say a word; don't ask me no mother fucken questions; you can't go to the bathroom; you can't do anything until I am finished stripping you of your dignity; if you don't like it, then don't bring your sorry, pathetic, low-life asses to prison. Jack wasn't appreciating his treatment at all. This CO was talking reckless, but at the end of the day, these were the people calling the shots. The CO went up and down the line doing his job. After it was all said and done, the new inmates were now ready for quarantine.

Tying up loose ends, Footty was standing outside of Louie's house whistling up at his window. Louie looked out the window and was happy to see Footty, so he opened the door and let him in. "Footty, where have you been? I have been worried sick about my car, you know I had to report it stolen so that the insurance company would pay for it, they haven't given me any money yet. They said they couldn't do anything until the investigation was finished on that guy who got killed in it."

"Wow, is that what they said? Who else did you talk to?"

"Nobody other than my insurance broker."

"And what did you tell him?"

"Not much, only that my car had been stolen the night before."

"Has anyone else been out here to talk to you."

"No."

"Are you sure, you wouldn't lie to me, now, would you?"

"Okay, okay, you got me, a light-skinned detective did come by and said his name was Mickey, or something."

"Oh really, keep going."

"He showed me a picture of the young boy who got killed, he also asked me had I ever seen him before."

"And what did you say?"

"I told him no, I never seen him in my life, for real, I wouldn't lie to you."

"I know you wouldn't you have always looked out for me, if you don't mind me asking, do you have anything to drink?"

"No, I do not, unless you want a cold glass of water."

"That will be fine." Footty and Louie walked into the kitchen. Louie opened the refrigerator and took out a gallon of ice-cold water and poured Footty a glass. Footty thanked Louie for the water then told him he was glad that he didn't bring his name up when the detective came by asking questions.

"Footty, you know how I roll; I would have never done that."

"I know, Louie, that's why I brought you a treat." Footty pulled out a quarter ounce of that hard manila.

Louie's eyes lit up, then he said, "Now that's what I'm talking about." He then reached into his pocket and poured out a straight shooter. "You know, Footty, that's why I love you so much, you always be looking out." Footty gave Louie the sandwich bag full of cocaine. Louie sat down at the kitchen table and started beaming up to Scotty. "Man, Footty, please tell me you got some more of this shit right here."

"Of course, I do, it is plenty more where that came from." Louie was getting fucked up, he was so high, he never saw Footty grab that butcher knife out of his dish rack. Louie put another big-ass rock into his pipe and put some fire to it. He was sucking on that straight shooter so hard that his face began to cave in. Footty pulled both shades down to Louie's kitchen windows. He then walked over to him and stabbed him in his neck. Louie let out a small scream and fell to the floor. Footty jumped down on top of him and started stabbing him to death. Blood was splashing all over the place, and Footty kept stabbing. "You won't open your mouth now, will you, motherfucker? As Footty stuck that ten-inch knife deep into Louise's chest, his adrenaline was pumping. He could feel it, each time he pushed that blade into his body. Footty continued poking holes in Louie until he completely stopped moving.

His office phone was ringing. It rang about six times before he picked it up. "Hello."

"What's up, captain?"

"Hey, what's going on O G Sun, how has life been treating you?"

"Good, but you know a nigga can always do better."

"What do I owe the honors of this call?"

"I need you to do O G Sun a big favor."

"Sure, anything, you name it."

"Are you anywhere near your computer?"

"Yes, I am, why?"

"Well, you just got a new prisoner in, and I need you to take care of him for me."

"Now, you know I can't do that, but I can tell you what I can do."

"And what is that?"

"I can have him sent to the worst block in the entire prison and put the word out, I'm pretty sure he will get stabbed, that's about all I can do."

"Alright, that's cool, then make it happen."

"And what is his name so I can look him up?"

"His name is Jack Parker."

The captain looked up Jack and saw that he still was in quarantine, so he moved them up on the list: his destination, A, 21. "Alright OG, it's done."

"Thanks captain, I owe you one."

"It's all good, anything for my son-in-law, you just keep taking good care of my daughter."

"No doubt, you know I got you."

"One love player, I'm out." The captain hung the phone up and didn't have a second thought about what he'd just done. He just put Jack's life in danger, but little did he know, danger was no stranger to BlackJack.

Jack had only been in quarantine for about six days when his name was called to go to population. He was sitting down in the day room watching TV when they told him to pack it up. He was being moved. Jack got his stuff and was told to wait in the sally port with about fourteen other people. The COs came on to the pod and grabbed each one of their face cards, then told the inmates to follow them. As they got to the end of the Hallway of B eleven, the fourteen other inmates went one way, and Jack went the other. The CO took Jack on to the elevator and got off on the second floor. He then took Jack's face card to the bubble. The bubble told him to take Jack to A, 21. Jack entered the pod and took his paperwork up to the COs desk. As the two CO's looked up, they almost shitted on themselves. Both knew Jack. Jack had previously shot one of them and smacked the shit out of the other. From that moment on, Jack had a G pass. Jack just stared at both, then one of the COs spoke up.

"Oh, um, Jack, is there any particular cell you would like to stay in?"

Jack said, "Yes, I want twenty-one cell." The CO got on the mic and told Jermaine Pratt, in 21 cell, to move his shit. Jack sat at the table and waited for Jermaine to move. As the blue tenants tried to come up front, the CO's told them to fall back. When Jermaine was done, Jack picked up his stuff, and walked to the top of the steps. He signaled to the CO to turn the TVs off. The inmates started snapping and told the COs to turn the fucken TVs back on. Jack said, "Yo, I need you to listen up, because I'm telling all you motherfucker's right now, if anyone of yall get out of pocket with me, I will knock you straight the fuck out." He then signaled back to the COs to turn the TVs back on. Niggas started talking shit as Jack went upstairs to his cell. When Jack walked in, he noticed his celly had taken the bottom bunk. The inmates were talking.

"Man, can you believe this fucking bitch-ass nigga, who do he think he is, don't he know he is about to get banged the fuck out?" All the so-called tough guys went and got strapped up.

Then one guy said, "I don't know who he thinks he is, but he sure do look familiar, I think I know him from somewhere." Jack came back down the steps and the COs called him over to their desk.

"Jack, please do us a favor, and chill."

Jack said, "One thing I don't do is listen to no fake-ass cops, if anything, you will listen to me. Now, tell me who runs this block, who is supposed to be mister Billy bad ass?" Both COs looked at each other, then back at Jack.

"His name is JD, from twelve cell." JD was lying in his cell sleep, until he heard his door buzz. He jumped up looking crazy, wondering who had enough balls to wake him the fuck up. See JD was a big, cocky-ass-African-looken motherfucker, with a big bald head, and was mean and nasty for no reason. All the inmates were in disbelief as they watched Jack make his way over to twelve cell. Jack popped JD's cell door open, then sucker punched the shit out of him without asking any questions. JD went crazy. He put his head down and rushed Jack, football tackling him out of the door and into the day room. Jack was like, "Okay, I got something for all this he-man shit." Jack slapped both of his hands across JD's ears, then he headbutted him in the nose. As JD fell to the side holding his face, Jack rolled over and stood up on his feet. JD got up and started swinging all wild. The crowd gathered around, and Jack was making his statement. For every one punch JD threw, Jack would hit him four to five times with precise combinations at blazing speeds. JD tried to rush Jack again. Jack grabbed him and brought down a crushing elbow to the back of his neck, sending JD crashing to the floor. JD tried to get back up, but Jack hit him with two ridiculous body blows. That made JD quit fighting. The COs ran over and told Jack and JD to cut it out. Jack put his hands down and walked off. The block was in shock. JD had been beating the shit out of niggas and taking their belongings ever since he came to the block. But not anymore. Jack was in his cell changing his shirt and washing the blood off his hands when he heard a slight tap on his door. Jack pushed his cell door open and saw a young man standing there. "Can I help you?" he said.

"Maybe you can, I didn't come here for any trouble, I just wanted to know if I could ask you a question."

"You sure can, I don't see why not?"

"Is your name BlackJack Parker?"

"Yes, but just call me Jack."

"And do you have a son by the name of Pooh Bear?"

Jack said, "Yes," again, and the young boy started jumping up and down.

"I knew it, I knew I knew you from somewhere."

Jack said, "A lot of people know me, but the question is, do I know you?"

The young boy said, "Yes, you know me, Mr. Parker, but you might not remember me, my name is Big Zeke, I was Pooh Bear's best friend as a kid when I lived out in Tasker until my parents moved me away."

It took Jack a few minutes, but he remembered exactly who he was. Jack invited Big Zeke into his cell so that they could talk. "Zeke, what are you doing in a place like this?"

"Well, Mr. Jack, it's a long story." "Okay, check this out, drop the Mister Jack shit, and just call me Jack, and the last time I checked, neither one of us is going anywhere, anytime soon, so let me here it."

"Alright then, I'm in here for murder."

"What?"

"Yes, that is what they are trying to pin on me."

"Was you there on the scene?"

"No."

"Can anybody point the finger at you?"

"No."

"Do they have any evidence against you?"

"No."

"Then how can they accuse you of murder?" Do you have a paid lawyer?"

"No, just a public defender."

"I don't mean to sound cruel, but you are fucked, do your parents have any money to get you a good lawyer?"

"No."

"Well how do they feel about your situation?"

"They don't feel any kind of way."

"And why not?"

"Well Mister, I mean Jack, both of my parents are dead." Silence filled the room. "That's why I am here."

"Because you killed your own parents?"

"I mean I did, and I didn't."

Jack said, "Hold up, back that shit up a little bit. You are telling me you did, but you didn't? What kind of shit is that? Now, you either going to come clean with me, or you can get the fuck out of my cell."

"Alright Jack, this is what happened. Me and my dad had an argument earlier that day, he had me real fucken mad at him. He just kept getting on my nerves about fixing the brakes on the car. He told me to stop being so fucken lazy, and I needed to get a job. I didn't really feel like working on no car because he had me so angry, so when I did put the brakes on, I forgot to put the pins back into the calipers, so later on that evening, when my mom and dad left out to go to dinner, the brakes failed, and they slid into oncoming traffic, going head up with a Mac truck. They were killed instantly."

"So you mean to tell me they are trying to say you sabotaged your own parents' car?"

"Yes, and they are trying to get me on murder one."

Jack knew that with a public defender, Big Zeke would be found guilty. Without a paid lawyer, this young boy didn't have a chance at winning his case. Jack's cell mate came upstairs and felt some type of way that Big Zeke was in his housing area. Jack told Zeke to excuse himself so he and his celly could talk. Jack closed the door behind Zeke, then turned around and trashed the shit out of his celly. He told him to never ever interrupt him again when he is talking. "And now that I think about it, when I come back from taking my shower, all your shit better be on that top bunk."

CHAPTER 16

M om Parker and Pooh Bear were sitting at the table eating dinner. It was a little strange without all three of them being there, but she fixed Jack a plate, anyway, every single day.

"Mom, have you heard from dad?"

"No, not yet, but I called the prison and they said they were moving him out of quarantine, so we should be hearing from him soon."

" Pooh Bear, I need you to come by the store today so you can go over the numbers and order forms for next week's shipment. I need your opinion on some new products that I want to sell in the store, then I need you to count the safe and make sure all the money is straight." Just then the phone rang. Pooh Bear answered it thinking it was his father, but it wasn't. It was Rudy Ray calling to find out what Jack's status was.

"Rudy, we haven't heard anything yet, but he should be calling soon. As soon as we hear anything, will call you back and give you the scoop, okay?"

"That sounds like a plan, and tell your mother that Deena said to call her whenever she gets a chance."

Pooh Bear said, "Alright, I will tell her." Then he hung up the phone.

The next morning came, Jack was up washing his face in the sink when he heard the CO announce that the pod was about to open. Jack brushed his teeth, then his hair, and put on his blue uniform shirt. He left out of his cell and went down the steps into the day room. Big Zeke was at the card table doing some card tricks. Jack walked up and turned the TV to what he wanted to watch, then sat down. Nobody said a damn thing. They just got up and went to watch the other TV. Jack put his feet up, chillin.' Big Zeke walked over and sat next to him, smiling.

Jack looked at him and said, "How you are doing today, young boy?"

"I'm chillin'."

"And what's up with that smile you got all over your face?"

"So, you haven't heard, that nigga JD got himself moved off of the block this morning."

"And why did he do that?"

"Oh, I don't know, your guess is as good as mine," Big Zeke started laughing, "and that's not all I heard, word is he checked into protective custody."

"Really?"

"Yes, really." Jack and Zeke continue to talk. Meanwhile, niggas were starting to hate on Zeke thinking he was on Jack's dick, not knowing Jack was his old head.

Rudy Ray had been doing double the amount of therapy he needed to get his leg as strong as possible, as quickly as he could. Somebody dropped the dime on Jack, and he had a small idea as to who it might be. If he was right about who he thought it was, they were about to be in for a rude awakening.

The whole backside of the day room belonged to Jack. He would be sitting there, day after day, watching TV. As the blue tenants brought him his food, the only one that could go over and sit with him was Big Zeke. As the pod would line up for the evening meal, some of the inmates wouldn't eat. They would just line up so they could be the first to use the phone. Now, the COs never turned the phones on until after all the inmates had eaten, unless Jack needed to use the phone. Jack and Big Zeke walked up to the front to use the phone. As Jack and Big Zeke approached the top, a small crowd follow them. The COs told all of them to get back in line and wait until the top was clear. Jack picked up the receiver and told the CO to tell the bubble to turn the phones back on. Jack put his Pp number in, then put in his home telephone number and the phone started ringing. Pooh Bear answered it.

"Hey dad."

"Hey what's up, son, where's your mother?"

"She is upstairs."

"Alright then, put her on the phone."

Pooh Bear yelled up the steps, telling his mother to come and get the phone. "Dad, can we come and see you?"

"Yes, but let me talk to your mother first, and don't you go anywhere because I have a surprise for you."

"A surprise?"

"Yes—"

Pooh Bear's mom snatched the phone out of his hand. "Hey baby, I have been missing you."

"I missed you too, my love."

"Can we come and visit you now?"

"You sure can."

"Good, I will be up there tomorrow morning. I already put a thousand dollars on your books. You have a letter and two cards coming to you in the mail."

"That's my girl."

"Honey, what's all that noise I hear in the background?" Jack told Tina to hold on, then he put the phone down, turned around and told everybody to shut the fuck up while he is talking to his wife. The whole pod went silent, even the COs.

"Sorry about that honey, now where was I? Oh yes, my visiting day is on Wednesday. If you come up before three pm, you can stay for an hour, if you come up after three, you can only stay for half."

"Jack, that is crazy, I can only come see you one day a week?"

"No honey, you can come see me any day of the week you want, from Monday through Friday, but you would only get a half an hour, unless it is on a Wednesday."

"Oh, okay, I get it now." Pooh Bear was standing off to the side, next to his mother, waiting for her to finish so he could find out what his surprise was. "Jack, do you need me to bring you any T-shirts, underwear, or socks?"

"No, you can't do that anymore, I will order me some off of commissary with the money you put on my books."

"Are you sure?"

"I'm sure, love you, baby."

"I love you, too Jack."

Tina gave Pooh Bear back the phone. "Alright Dad, what is the surprise?"

 Jack passed the phone to Big Zeke. "What's up, Playboy?"

"Who is this?"

"Who do you think it is, long time no hear from?"

"Yo, I said who is this?"

"It is your boy."

Pooh Bear was getting mad at this nigga on the phone for not telling him who he was, but he knew if his dad put him on the phone, he had to be important. "My boy, I don't have no boy."

"Oh, you don't?"

"No, I don't."

"Damn, that just hurt my feelings."

"Your feelings? Man, who the fuck is this?"

"Calm down, I will give you a hint."

"Okay, what's the hint?"

"Remember when that big dude took our ball?"

"Our ball, what the fuck are you talking about?"

"Then I told him I would give him one chance to give us our kick ball back?" When Big Zeke said kick ball, it all came back to him.

"Oh, shit, is this who I think it is?"

"Yes, it's me."

"What's the deal, son? How have you been?"

"Things have been a little rough for me, but other than that, I'm good."

"How long have you been locked up?"

"Shit, I don't know, maybe a little over a year and a half."

"Wow, that long?"

"Yes, and I go to trial at the end of next month."

"*You now have sixty seconds,*" said the operator.

"Big Zeke, check this out, give me your first and last name, and your PP number, I will put some money on your books and send you out a letter."

"Damn, is it like that?"

"It sure is, I got you." Then Big Zeke's time ran completely out. When Jack and Big Zeke were done using the phone, that's when all the other inmates were allowed to get on and call their loved ones.

Home sweet home, Pooh Bear pulled up to 1801 Vine Street and parked his car. He went inside the courthouse and proceeded to room 31C. Today was the day that Bay Boy was supposed to be coming home. All he had to do was go in front of the judge and show him that he had gotten his GED, and the judge promised to let him go. Pooh Bear sat down and waited. There were a few stupid cases before they brought Bay Boy out. Bay boy stood in front of the judge. The judge started talking to him, everything the judge said went in one ear and right out the other, until he got to the part that he was releasing him. Pooh Bear was happy and so was Bay Boy. When the judge was done, Bay boy was free to go home. Pooh Bear and Bay Boy drove back to Pooh Bear's house. They walked in the front door, and Bay Boy said hi to mom Parker. Mom Parker spoke back, asking him how he has been, and that she was glad to see him. Pooh Bear and Bay Boy went upstairs to his room. Pooh Bear had six bags of clothes on his bed, three boxes of sneakers, and a pair of timberland boots, all for his man. He gave him a knot full of money, then went into his closet to get his present. Pooh Bear gave Bay Boy the box with a single bow on it.

"What is this?" Bay Boy said.

"Open it up and see for yourself."

Bay boy opened his present that Pooh Bear promised to give him, and he liked what he saw. "Is this for me?"

"Yes, and it's all yours?"

"What is it?"

"It is a forty cal; it will stop an elephant dead in his tracks."

Bay boy slid the clip in and out, then back and forth, *click click*, sliding a bullet into the chamber.

"So, are we going to move on these mother fuckers tonight?"

"No, we will have plenty of time for that, just take your stuff and go home and see your mom. She is wondering where you are."

"And here, I almost forgot this cell phone is for you, too. Lock my number in, and I will call you later tonight."

It was visiting day, and Jack was sitting on his bottom bunk, all dressed and ready to go. He was reading the newspaper to find out what was going on in the world. He could see the clock from his cell door window. It read eight fifty-five. Jack knew in five minutes they would be calling him for his visit. So, he brushed his teeth, then checked himself out in the mirror. His baby was coming to see him, and he had to look good. As soon as nine o'clock hit, the CO came over the loudspeaker and said, "Jack Parker, twenty-one cell, you have a visit." Then he buzzed Jack's door. Jack walked up to the CO's desk and grabbed his pass. He tucked in his shirt and walked into the sally port. The CO in the bubble buzzed the other door to let Jack out. One of the rovers stopped him and asked where he was going.

"I am going to a visit."

The rover checked his pass, then told him to turn around and put his arms up so that he could check him. Jack just looked at him real crazy. The rover said, "You know what, don't even worry about it, just go and enjoy your time with your family."

Jack made his way to the elevator, down to the first floor. As he sat in the tank for about twenty-five minutes, he just listened to all these so-called gangsters telling their war stories. Most of them were still wet behind the ears and had no idea that the stupid shit they were pulling down here would get them killed upstate. Jack heard keys on the other side of the door. The CO came in and called for forty-four, forty-five, forty-six, and forty-seven. Jack was number forty-seven. He gave him his slip, then went and changed his clothes. He walked up to the clothes window and asked for a 4X jumper. Jack put on his carrot suit, then walked out on the dance floor. The CO checked his armband and assigned him to seat five two. Forty-five minutes later, mom Parker and Pooh Bear walked into the visiting room, handed their passes to the guard at the desk, then walked over to where Jack was. Jack stood up and hugged his son, and kissed his wife, then they all sat down.

Collection day. E-money was out collecting his and Footty's money.

He pulled up to Louie's house and blew his horn. Normally, when E-money would blow his horn, Louie would always come out and pay his tab, especially at the first of the month. But this time, Louie never came out. So, E-money got out of his car and was about to knock on his door, when one of the young guys from around the way said, "Excuse me, but Mr. Louie is not home."

E- money said, "Well when he comes back, tell him I came by looking for him."

The young boy said, "He won't be coming back."

"And why not?"

"Because he's dead, somebody stabbed him to death the other day."

"Are you fucken serious?"

"Yes, I'm serious, I was out here the day when they brought him out, all zipped up in a black bag, and then put him in the back of a van."

E- money was like "Damn, who the fuck would want to hurt Louie, Louie wouldn't hurt a fly." E-money pulled out his cell phone and called Footty.

"Footty, you are not going to believe this."

"I'm not going to believe what?"

"Somebody just killed Louie."

"Get the fuck out of here, who would do such a thing?"

"I don't know, but whoever did it is a real fucken coward. Louie wasn't a threat to no one, that's fucked up."

"Real fucked up, E-money. Alright then partner, let me get back to collecting this money, I will see you when I am done, peace out."

Jack's visit. "So, how is everything going?"

"Everything is straight, Dad, the store is making good money, all the bills are paid on time, and the bread that was owed to you has been paid in full. The numbers look good, it's all of what you left, plus about twenty-five percent."

"Okay, that's great, way to stay on top of things. Tina, have you heard anything from JP Walker, yet?"

"Yes, he called me right back as soon as I called him. I told him what happened, he said he would jump right on it and come to see you ASAP."

"That would be nice."

"Dad, Bay Boy just came home, and Rudy Ray wants to know how you are doing, and do you need him to do anything for you."

"Tell Rudy Ray that we got a lot to talk about, but it won't be over none of these telephones, he must come visit me, once he fully recovers. Jack and his family continued to talk, until the visit was over.

Happy to see you. Pooh Bear just got off the phone with Carmen telling her Bay Boy was home. Carmen was ecstatic telling him she was going to order some pizza. Carmen asked him to bring Bay Boy over so they all could chill. Pooh Bear took the phone away from his mouth and asked Bay Boy did he want to go over to Carmen's.

Bay boy said, "I don't know, is Chippy over there?"

"She sure is."

"Then tell Carmen we are on our way."

Pooh Bear got back on the phone and told Carmen they would be right over. When Pooh Bear and Bay Boy got there, the pizza was still hot. They dug right in. Chippy and Carmen went to the kitchen.

Chippy was like, "Damn Carmen, do you see how fucken big Bay Boy dun got?"

"Yes, and he's a lot more handsome than I can remember."

"Shit, Carmen, you don't know it yet, but he is going to get some of this pussy tonight."

"Girl you crazy."

"No, I'm not, I'm just hornier than a motherfucker."

Both girls went back into the living room. A few minutes later Mya came over. When she saw Baby Boy, she jumped up and down, ran over to him, and gave him a big hug.

"All Bay Boy, it's good to see you, when did you get home?"

"I came yesterday."

"Yesterday, did you get some pussy, yet?"

"No, not yet."

"But he is about to." Chippy butted in. Bay Boy turned and looked at Chippy.

"I am?"

"Yes," as she grabbed his hand and led him up the steps. Bay Boy went upstairs with Chippy; Pooh Bear stayed downstairs and fucked the shit out of Carmen and Mya.

Not today. Big Zeke was cleaning out his cell, when he noticed a small crowd gathering by the showers staring over at him. The area where Jack sat was empty and the block was a little too quiet. Big Zeke knew something was up, so he walked upstairs to check on Jack, making sure everything was all good with him. But 21 cell was empty. Jack, or his cell mate wasn't in there. Then he remembered, oh, that's right, Jack had a visit today. So, he walked back down the steps and leaned up against the wall. Now the crowd had gotten a lot bigger. Big Zeke knew they were getting ready to move on him, but he didn't give a fuck, it is, what it is. As the crowd began to move in Big Zeke's direction, Jack walked back on to the block and peeped the whole scene. Jack saw them moving in on Zeke, and saw Zeke locked in on them. Jack handed the CO his visitor's pass, then walked over to Zeke and asked him if he was ready. "Ready as I'll ever be." Jack and Big Zeke walked over to the crowd; not one of them looked Jack in his face.

Jack responded, "Is there a problem here?"

"Not with you, Jack, but we do with that dick rider over there."

"Who are you calling a dick rider?"

"You, you are a dick rider."

"Do you want a piece of me?"

"I sure do."

Jack told everybody to chill the fuck out. "And let me tell you dum, mother fuckers something, if you got a problem with him, you got a problem with me, now, if you want some one-on-one shit, then let's have it."

"Say no more." Big Zeke stepped up and so did the nigga that was talking shit. Both put their hands up and started mixing it up. See, the nigga talking shit had no idea that Big Zeke hit harder than a son of a bitch. Big Zeke hit him with two punches in his arm and both spots frogged the fuck up. He started to run. He threw a wild haymaker, Big Zeke ducked it and hit him with a bone-crushing-body blow. The nigga talking shit dropped his hands, grabbed his stomach, and started throwing up all over the day room. Jack then pointed at three niggas in the front of the crowd, and said, "You, you, and you, got exactly one hour to check the fuck in. Twenty minutes later, all three of those niggas were headed to protective custody.

Stepping it up. Rudy Ray was getting stronger as each day passed by. Every afternoon after his therapy, he would go down to the shooting range and practice shooting all the latest handguns. He didn't really like them, but he knew he had to switch his style up because trying to run around, with a six-shot-riot pump, on one leg, wasn't going to cut it. His aim was getting good, and he was really starting to like that three-fifty-seven-snub nose with the rubber grip. He liked it so much that he bought himself one. He was going to find out who was snitching on Jack, even if it killed him.

Jack was out in the yard, getting his daily work out in, when the CO called his name. He told him that he had an official visit. Jack went and took a shower, then he put some fresh blues on. He got his pass, then rolled out. This time when Jack got to the holding tank, there was nobody in there. So, he handed his pass to the CO and was told to come into the back because his lawyer was in room 11. Jack walked into room 11, and low and behold, there he was—the great JP Walker.

"Jack, have a seat and shut the door." Jack shook JP's hand and sat down. "Alright, now, tell me, what is going on, your wife called and told me a little bit, but not enough, so I pulled your file, it said you are being charged with three counts of murder."

"I know, but I didn't kill anybody. That date they are saying this happened, I was home with my wife, and we stayed together the whole entire day."

"Will she testify to that on the witness stand in a courtroom if there is a district attorney in there?"

"Of course, she would."

"That's good to know, but right now it is too early to really know anything, I can't put any strategy's together until I get your discovery."

"And when will you be getting that?"

"Right after your preliminary hearing, which is in two more weeks. Then you will have an arraignment, then a second one, that's when I will know exactly what kind of evidence, they have against you."

"Look, JP, they shouldn't have any evidence on me because I didn't kill anybody.''

"Be patient, Jack, I'm on it, oh, and just so you know, I'm already paid in full. That's really all I have right now, I just wanted to touch base with you. Now that I have, you have any questions?"

"No, I don't have any questions for myself, but what I do have is some more work for you. I need you to pick up a case for me." Jack gave his lawyer Big Zeke's name and his PP number and told him all about his situation. He also told him that he would call and arrange for Tina to pay him for Big Zeke.

JP Walker said, "Thank you, I really appreciate it, I will be in touch."

CHAPTER 17

Have you seen my hommie? Bay Boy had been home for five days now. He had not seen or heard from Ra Ra, so he stopped by Ra Ra's house, but nobody was ever home. He checked all the parks and all the playgrounds, but there was no sign of his man. He called Pooh Bear.

"Yo, Pooh Bear, have you seen Ra Ra, I went past his house a few times and got no answer? Is there something you're not telling me?"

"No, not really, I told you everything in a letter that I sent you. Ra Ra hasn't been the same since Sheema got shot and she lost their twins, he seems to not know any of us. I have been trying to help him, but he doesn't want my help, whenever I see him walking the streets, I give him food and clothes, and he won't take it. Every other day, I ride around until I find him and make sure that he is alright, I haven't been able to find him in the last few days."

"Well, where do he be the most?"

"He be all over the place, walking the streets, day in and day out, I'm hoping that he comes back around, I be really missing him."

"Yes, me too, he doesn't even know I am home."

"I know, I tell you what, get dressed, and I will come pick you up, and we will go and find him."

Big Zeke was standing outside of Jack's cell when his name was called for a visit. "A visit?" he thought, "who the hell would be coming to visit me?" He got his pass and went to the visiting room. A few minutes later, Pooh Bear walked in the door. Big Zeke was happy to see him. Pooh Bear walked over and gave him a strong handshake and hug.

"Damn, Pooh Bear, you done got tall as shit."

"And you done got big as shit, what are they feeding you in here, other than dog food?"

"Nothing really, I just be going to the gym working out."

"I thought we might never see each other again, but here we are."

"Life is crazy the way shit be happening."

"So, what's good with you, Zeke?"

"On the up and up."

"Shit is really hectic out there, I'm at war with these cats from the Wilson projects, and it's the real deal."

"Man, sorry to hear that, if I was home, I will put an end to it for you, but the way shit looking now, I may never see the streets again."

"Stop stressing, Zeke, your case is not as bad as you think it is."

"Yes, it is."

"No, it's not."

"And how do you know that?"

"I just know, my dad hired you a lawyer, and your lawyer said you should beat your case." Big Zeke's eyes swelled up; he couldn't believe what he was hearing. His oldhead was looking out for him.

"Pooh Bear, I don't know what to say."

"You don't need to say anything, that's what friends are for. I just put five hundred dollars on your books and sent you a couple of double XL magazines, and when you get out, I have a present for you, also."

Big Zeke was speechless for a moment, then he said, "Pooh Bear, from this day on, my loyalty is with you, until death do us part."

Pooh Bear and Bay boy were riding around the last few hours trying to find Ra Ra, when Bay Boy's phone rang. It was Chippy.

"Hey baby, what are you doing?"

"Me and Pooh Bear is out looking for Ra Ra."

"Oh, that's good, when you are done, can you please come over to Carmen's house and see me, I'm missing you?"

"I sure can, as a matter of fact, we are on our way."

In no time, Pooh Bear and Bay Boy were pulling up in front of Carmen's. They both got out and went into the house. Both Carmen and Chippy were sitting on the couch watching the Maury Povich show. All you could hear was "you are not the father." Pooh Bear said, "Why do you girls like watching this garbage?" then walked over and turned the TV. Carmen threw a pillow at him and told him to turn it back. Pooh Bear told her to hush, as he turned the volume up on the news. The news reporter was talking about a man named Louie More, who had been stabbed to death at his home right on the outskirts of the Wilson projects. Then she said, "There was an unidentified-black male, found dead, floating in the Schoolkill River, and all evidence point to an apparent suicide. A witness said she seen a black male standing on the other side of the bridge, she then said she tried to save him, but he just looked up at the sky, then back at her smiling like he had just found peace with himself, then he jumped. If anybody have an idea who this person is," then she flashed a picture across the screen, "please call, 2 6 7 5 5 5 1 0 1 0 right away." Chippy jumped up off the couch and started screaming and crying. "Oh my God, yall, that's Ra Ra on that picture." Carmen started to gag and cough; she was choking over her own words. Pooh Bear held on tight to Bay Boy to try and calm him down as guilt began too way heavy on him. Ra Ra was dead, could he have done more to save him?

Commissary day. Jack was sitting in the day room, doing him, when he heard the CO callout, "commissary up." Big Zeke still was asleep. He normally didn't get up until about one or two in the afternoon because he worked overnight, as the eleven to seven re therm worker, but sleep or no sleep, it was something about the call of commissary that would wake a nigga up. A female CO named, Micah, called Jack's name. Jack got up and went up top for his bag. As he walked past the CO, she was like "Damn, that black-ass-chocolate nigga smell good as shit," as her eyes followed him over to the table where he was making sure he had all his items that he had ordered. Jack saw her checking him out, so he grabbed his dick. She was thinking to herself, "Wow, I can see this nigga print through his pants, I know this mother fucker's packen." Jack took his stuff to his cell then went back and sat down in the day room. When the CO finished calling commissary, she went into the bathroom and played with herself until she came.

Choices we make. "So, what do we do now, is this shit over, or what?"

"Fuck no, this shit ain't over until those faggot-ass niggas out in Tasker is dead."

"I don't know if you have noticed, but there has been a lot of blood shedding over the past year."

"Don't tell me you are going soft on me, E-money."

"No, not at all, but since Ra Ra is dead, don't you think we should let this shit die down?"

"Man, only thing I'm going to let die is Pooh Bear, bitch ass, when I see him. Them niggas out in Tasker killed Apple, remember?"

"Yes, I remember, how can I forget, I have a picture of all of us on my wall as soon as you walk into my room. It looks like we are winning the war, they have lost three, and we only lost two."

"Yes, but I heard that fat-bastard, Bay Boy, just came home."

"Is that supposed to mean something?"

"Of course, it means they are reloading. You know Ra Ra was his right-hand man."

"Shit, then we need to reload, too."

"Exactly, now you are getting my point, I want to stab Pooh Bear in his heart so bad and watch him die."

"Damn, you must really hate that nigga."

"I sure do, like a fat bitch would hate a diet, I just don't like that mother fucker."

"I don't like him, either."

"I guess that gives us more of a reason to want to kill him, even if it's the last thing I do." Footty took two quick snorts of dope.

"Man, why do you keep sniffing that shit, don't you know you not supposed to get high off your own supply?"

"This is not my own supply, it's my personal supply." Footty laughed. E-money just shook his head as they both chilled for the rest of the day.

Slick captain. The captain was sitting in the bubble all day long watching Jack. The COs had already told him that the captain was on his top, so Jack played it cool. He worked out in the yard, then took a shower. He shared the telephones and wasn't on none of his boss shit that he usually be on. The captain was getting mad and frustrated that he couldn't catch Jack doing anything wrong. So, he went into the computer and looked up the most dangerous inmate he had in the entire prison, then had him released from the hole with specific instructions to send him straight to Jack's housing area. The captain left out of the bubble just a laughing and giggling, but at the end of the day, who was going to get the last laugh?

The aftermath. Ra Ra's funeral was the saddest of them all. There wasn't a dry eye in the whole entire funeral home. As Pooh Bear, Bay Boy, and four other gentlemen carried Ra Ra's casket to the hearse that was waiting outside, Pooh Bear and Bay Boy knew this was the last time they would ever see their friend. After all the cars got to the cemetery, Sheema was the first to get out and stand over Ra Ra's casket before they lowered him into the ground. As the preacher started to read some more scriptures, everybody that walked by his casket laid a beautiful red rose on top of it. The choir began singing, "He is going up to yonder, to be with the Lord." The preacher released two-white doves in the memory of this young man. Tears began to flow as they lowered Ra Ra into his grave six feet beneath the earth. On the ride back home, Bay Boy was completely silent. He just kept biting on his nails and shaking his head. As Chippy tried to cheer him up, Pooh Bear was becoming numb to these situations. He had lost three hommies in one year, and now it was time for some payback.

It was three thirty in the morning when Big Zeke heard the CO's keys dangling outside of his cell door. Today was the day. Instead of him going to work, he was going to court. The CO opened his door and told him to get ready. Big Zeke took his shower, got dressed, and ate himself some breakfast as he sat in the day room talking to other inmates who had court that day, too. They sat talking until they heard the bubble call "all courts to the sally port." There were about twenty-five people in total from all the surrounding pods. The CO said, "It's time to roll out," as everyone headed to the elevators, stepping on, then stepping off, piling into a small holding cell. Soon, one by one, each inmate's name was called. They could get their clothing bag to change their clothes. Within the hour, the sheriffs arrived and prepared the inmates to be transported. As they searched everyone, they handcuffed them again in pairs of twos, loaded them up on the prison bus, and off to c j c they went. As the bus pulled into a big garage, they were unloaded and put back onto an elevator headed up to the second floor. They entered another cell that opened from both sides, and it was cold as a mother fucker in there. Big Zeke was glad that he thought ahead and brought his long john shirt. Suddenly, the opposite side door opened and two more sheriffs came in and unhandcuffed everybody, saying, "Now, I need you to follow my instructions, step out of this cell, and line up against that wall, take off your belts, and drop them right there on the floor, and walk through that metal detector, when you get through to the other side, grab yourself a cheese sandwich and two juices from out of those crates, then, you see those cells, at the end of the hall, start filling them up. Big Zeke was nervous; he didn't know what to expect; he sat there quietly. He listened to all these young boys laughing and joking like this shit was a game, like they were about to pass go and get two hundred dollars. They were going to get something, and it had nothing to do with money. CJC only dealt in years.

There were about fifteen people left in Big Zeke's cell. Seven of them went upstairs laughing and came back down crying like babies. Fifteen to thirty, twenty-five to fifty, thirty to sixty, the judge passed out years, and the inmates passed out tears. Big Zeke heard his name over the loudspeaker. It was time to pick twelve, Zeke and JP Walker picked six and the district attorney picked the rest. For the next seven days, the DA and JP Walker fought it out in court. It was a knockdown-dirty fight and JP was winning. The DA wanted the jury to believe that Big Zeke killed his own parents, but JP Walker wasn't having it. On the seventh, and final day, the jury rested, and JP and Big Zeke waited on the verdict. After the jury finished deliberating, a verdict was reached. The bailiff handed the verdict to the jury box. The judge asked them if they were ready and the jury said, "Yes." "Alright then, let's hear it." A lady stood up from the jury and said, "Your Honor, we the jury have reached our verdict. We find the defendant, Ezekiel L. Lions," there was a small pause, "not guilty." Big Zeke fell to his knees and began to cry. He couldn't believe he had just won his case. In a few hours, he would be a free man to have a second chance on life. Big Zeke went back to the block after court. Jack was sitting in his usual spot. Zeke walked over to him with happiness all over his face. Jack never even looked up from reading his newspaper.

"So, you will be leaving us sometime tonight, I guess?"

"How do you know, I haven't told you anything, yet?"

"You didn't have to. I put JP Walker on your case and all he do is win."

Zeke sat there speechless. "Jack, I just wanted to say thank you, I don't know how I could ever repay you."

"Look young-in, what I did for you was a small thing. Don't sweat it, I talked to my wife already and told her to prepare a room for you, and that you will be coming there to stay. Pooh Bear will take it from there and get you anything else you need."

"But Jack—"

Jack just waved his hands. Big Zeke didn't say another word, he just sat there and listened to Jack finish schooling him. The next morning, Big Zeke was told to pack his belongings because he was being released. Just before he left, he walked past Jack's cell and gave him a handshake and a hug.

"You be safe, young scrappy, I'll see you out there soon, now, get your ass out of here." Big Zeke picked his bags up and gave them to the guy in the cell next to Jack because he didn't need any of it. The CO called Big Zeke told him to hurry up and leave off the premises. As soon as Big Zeke walked off the pod, Omar came on to it, right from the hole.

Scot-free. Big Zeke left c f c f for the first time in almost 2 years. All he had was a pink slip and a token. As he stood on the bus stop waiting on the bus, Pooh Bear and Bay Boy pulled up, blowing their horn. "Yo, hommie, are you going somewhere?"

Big Zeke looked in the car and said, "Oh, shit, what's up, anyone going my way?"

"No, not really, but if you got a couple of dollars, I will drop you off wherever you need to go."

"A couple of dollars? All I got for you is a token, how far would that get me?"

"Not that far." Big Zeke laughed, dropped his token, ran over to the car, and got in.

"Welcome to the jungle." Pooh Bear said, as he sped off with his tires screeching.

Omar was in the multipurpose room planning his attack on Jack. He was up all night sharpening his whack. He was only on the pod for a few minutes, and he already had a few flunkies piping him up, but Omar didn't need any help getting hype. He was already throwed the fuck off. He was one sick dude and had just spent the last eighteen months in the hole for kicking a CO in his ass. He had six more months to go but was let go early to do somebody a favor. Jack could easily see how these soft-ass niggas were acting around Omar, so he knew Omar must have carried some weight. He needed to keep a close eye on him. It was about one o'clock on a Sunday afternoon. The Eagles game was about to come on. Jack was staring in his mirror and cracking his neck back and forth. He slid on his blue pants and put his boots on instead of his sneakers. "Yes, I think it's about time to break these bad boys in." He grabbed his shirt, pulled it over his head, then he grabbed a towel and wet it, threw it over his shoulder, then he walked out of the cell, back down into the day room, over to his favorite spot, he turned the game on, and sat down. "This is strange," he said, "it is a quarter after one, and the blue tenants haven't brought me my lunch, yet." All types of red flags went up, but Jack continued to sit there, in the middle of the gray-plastic-cushion chairs. The Eagles were beating the Cowboys. Omar slid out of the multipurpose room on some real sneaky shit. Jack was looking at him out the corner of his eye. Omar walked up, stood behind him, then slipped his banger from under his shirt. Everybody at the card table saw what he was about to do, but they just kept playing cards. Omar spun around and tried to stab Jack. Jack quickly moved to the side as the six-inch knife stabbed deep down into the top of the chair. Jack grabbed the banger and said, "You missed me motherfucker." Handing it back to him, "Now, do you want to try that shit again?" Omar raised his banger, and swung it again. Jack dipped it and hit him with a devastating right cross. Jack's fists must have had NyQuil all over them because Omar went straight to sleep. Two niggas tried to rush Jack from the crowd, but he tossed both to the side, then kicked the shit out of Omar. Omar started to regain consciousness and tried to pick himself up. Jack kicked him again right in his face. Omar jumped up and started swinging all wild with his banger. He was barely missing Jack. One of the guys who tried to rush Jack, tried to trip him, so Jack busted his nose wide open. Just as Jack hit the boy in the crowd, Omar stabbed him in his arm. Jack circled back around and grabbed his towel that he dropped on the floor and started twirling it. Then Jack started aiming it at the knife in Omar's hand letting it pop until he finally hit it. The banger flew up into the air and out of Omar's hand, falling in the day room. Omar tried to pick it up, but Jack rushed him, knocking him through the shower doors and into the shower. Jack reached up and turned the water on and tried to drown his mother fucken ass. Jack just kept saying, "This son of a bitch is strong as a fucken ox." The COs ran up, told Jack and Omar to stop, and sprayed both with pepper spray. Jack and Omar ate that shit and kept on rumbling. Jack's arm was bleeding bad, so he stepped back, hit Omar with a four-piece combination, side stepped him, and followed it up with the overhand right and two body blows. Omar fell to one knee, grabbed Jack, and they started tussling back and forth, throwing each other on top of the card table, breaking it, as they went crashing to the floor. Omar punched and tried to bite Jack, but Jack was hammering away at his rib cage. The CO pepper sprayed them again and it had no effect. The captain and the cert team ran on to the pod. The captain told the cert team to stand down and let them finish. Omar rolled over and got on top of Jack, hitting him with two good punches to his jaw, Jack covered his face up as Omar tried to land two more. Jack hit him with three-real-hard-body shots, then grabbed and headbutted the shit out of him. Omar's right eye split open, leaking all over the place. Jack rolled over and got up, and so did Omar. They started dancing again. Jack was bobbing and weaving, tagging the shit out of Omar's face. Omar picked up one of the plastic chairs and threw it at Jack. Jack punched the chair out of the air. Omar rushed him again. Jack hit him with two vicious uppercuts. He stumbled to the side right next to his banger, and he picked it up, quickly stabbing Jack in his shoulder blade. Jack pushed Omar away and slid the banger out of his shoulder. Jack looked at Omar then licked the blood off the knife. Now, Jack was really pissed. His eyes turned bloodshot red, and the look of death was upon his face. Jack moved in for the kill. That's when the captain told the CERT team to break it up. Jack backed up and dropped the banger, but Omar wasn't trying to hear that shit. Jack had just beat his ass and he didn't like it, not one bit. The CERT team gripped Omar up. "Get the fuck off of me and let me kill this motherfucker." The CERT team wouldn't let him go, so Omar snapped the fuck out and sucker punched both of them. Then he went after the captain. "Call off your dog's so I can finish what you asked me to do." Jack looked at the captain with confusion on his face. The CERT team grabbed Omar and slammed his head into the yard window. Omar was dazed. He shook it off and kicked one of the CERT team members in his stomach, then put him in a head lock while still swinging at the other. Omar was getting punched, and pepper sprayed in his face at the same time, but he wouldn't let that CO go. Jack was sitting back watching Omar get his ass kicked. They were spraying so much pepper spray, the inmates that were locked in their cells were choking. Omar was dragging the CO by his neck, trying to get away from that spray. Then all you heard was the COs neck snap then his body went limp. The other CERT team member tackled Omar down the steps, slamming is head and his face back and forth to the floor, until all his teeth fell out. Then one CO sat on top of him, one was hog-tying him, while the other was stomping Omar's face, until you heard his neck snap, then he stopped moving. The COs then got up and when after Jack. Jack turned around and surrendered, he put his hands behind his back and the CERT team handcuffed him, and started roughing him up. Jack just kept staring at the captain; the captain knew this shit had gotten way out of hand; he had one dead inmate, and worst of all, one dead CO. It was on his watch, and he was gonna make Jack pays for it, so he thought, anyway. "Take his monkey ass to the hole and throw away the fucking key." Jack walked by the captain, with a CERT team member on each arm, and as soon as he got close enough, he hawks spit right in his face, then said, "Oh, and by the way, you can kiss my ass," as he was being taken away.

CHAPTER 18

B ig Zeke was in his new room, getting all squared away, when Pooh Bear walked in with his present that he promised to give him when he got home.

"Is that for me?"

"It sure is."

Big Zeke opened it up. "Wow, this thing right here, is nice."

Bay Boy said, "Yes, we know, we all got one. See look," pulling his gun out. Then Pooh Bear showed his gun, too.

"Shit, with all this firepower, what are we going to do with it?"

Pooh Bear said, "We are going to make some fucken noise, we move on them nigga's tonight."

That shit was music to Bay Boy's ears. He was about to get some payback. Pooh Bear pulled a black duffel bag out of the closet; in it was black pants, black long-sleeved shirts, black mask, black gloves, and black boots. Then he pulled out a suitcase, and in it, was, all types of ammunition and five-bulletproof vests. We will wait until nightfall, then we will get this party started, quickly. Pooh Bear and his boys prepared for the point of no return.

Rudy Ray was out pounding the pavement, following every lead he had gotten. The information that Jack was sending him in his letters were all leading to dead ends. Then Rudy Ray remembered the conversation him and Jack had at the hospital about Duck, so he decided to pay him a visit. *knock knock knock, knock knock, knock* Duck came to the door, shocked to see Rudy Ray standing on his doorsteps.

"Rudy, what's up, how have you been, what brings you to my part of town?"

"Well, quite a few things, do you have a few minutes to talk?"

"Now is not a good time, Rudy, try me around the same time tomorrow." Then he went to close the door, but Rudy Ray put his foot in the door and stopped Duck from closing it. Duck already had his gun out behind the door.

"It's about Jack, we need to talk right now." Duck had a look of concern on his face.

"What about Jack, is he okay?"

"I don't know, you tell me." Duck put away his gun, opened the door, and let Rudy Ray into his house.

It's time. "E-money, word is, another one of Pooh Bear's soldiers done came home, that brings them back up to three."

"Damn dog, they are almost back to full strength."

"I know, we can't let that happen, what are we going to do?"

"We are going to have to hit them."

"When?"

"Now, like today. You ready?"

"Yes, I'm ready, did you pick up that stuff we ordered?"

"Of course, I got it, it's right here in the trunk."

E-money opened his trunk. Footty was pleased, he reached in and pulled out a brand-new, AR-15 with the beam, and right next to it was an AK-47. "Now, this is what I am talking about, these bitches won't know what hit them, until it's too late." Footty stood there smiling, he didn't give a fuck that Ra Ra killed himself, he wanted to kill somebody for killing Apple. So, one of these other niggas was going to have to do. "E-money, meet me back here after the sun goes down. We hit them, tonight."

Falling back. The captain needed this heat to go away, quickly, so he picked up the phone and called his son in law. "Hello, father-in-law, it's good to hear from you. Is my little problem taken care of?"

"No, not yet."

"Well, what the fuck is taking you so long?"

"He hasn't been so easy to get."

"I have figured that part out already, tell me something I don't know."

"Well, what is your next move going to be?"

"There is no next move."

"And why not?"

"Because we have a big fucken problem, some people got killed trying to get at his ass, so right now, there is a huge investigation going on. So don't call me again until this is over, I will only call you. Until then, I need you to fall back, and let me handle this mess."

"Captain, if you don't mind me asking, where is he now?"

"I locked him in the hole with no release date and suspended all of his visiting privileges." OG Son found that shit real funny. "Good, and don't feed that motherfucker, either."

"I won't, and I'm going to turn off the water to his cell." Both men were cracking the fuck up, hanging up on each other.

Nightfall. Pooh Bear, Bay Boy, and Big Zeke were all geared up. Mom Parker was laid on the couch hard asleep, as the boys quietly snuck past her and went out the backdoor. Pooh Bear had a black van parked in the cut, they all got in and went over their plan. Pooh Bear then said, "Anyone that's not willing to go all the way, get out of the van, right now." Nobody moved. "Alright then, let's do it. Weapons: check, check, bulletproof vest: check, check, ammo: check, check, black mask: check, check, extra clip: check, check, heart, and balls: check, check. okay then, we out, destination, the Wilson Park projects."

Double plated. Pooh Bear had been planning his attack for a long time. He was just waiting for the right moment, and the moment was right. He had a lot of work done on that van. The inside of it was layered with extra three-inch-thick steel, with a Porsche 9 1 1 engine in it just in case they had to make a quick getaway or get caught up in a high-speed chase. Finally, they reached their destination and all they saw walking around were dope fiends and prostitutes. Pooh Bear turned off his headlights as they circled around the projects, then he looked off to his left side and saw two men loading weapons into the back of a trunk. Pooh Bear came to a complete stop to get a better look, and those guys were exactly who they were looking for—Footty and E-money. The boys slid the van door open quietly, trying not to make any noise, but Footty noticed the strange van parked in the middle of the street, so he alerted E-money. "Yo, E, who the fuck is that?"

He whispered, "I don't know, I have never seen that van around here before."

"Me either." Footty reached into the trunk and pulled out the AK-47. Just then, they saw two men run into position, then shots rang out, *block ah, block ah, block ah, block ah, block ah, block block, block ah,boom, boomboom,boom,boomboomboomboom,boomboom,* Footty and E-money ducked down,*boomboomboom,block ah, block ah*, bullets were ricocheting off the grill on the front of their car. Footty took a deep breath, then came up cutting loose. *wopwopwopwopwopwopwopwopwopwopwop,wopwop,* That AK-47 was rocking that van back and forth, *wopwopwopwopwop,* the windows were busted out. Pooh Bear ran to the other end of the van, returning fire *,block ah, block ah, block ah, block block ah, block ah, block ah,* e money said, now it's my turn,*rat tat tat tat tat tat tat tat tat tat,rat tat tat tat tat tat, wopwopwopwopwopwopwopwopwop,boomboomboom,block* *ah, block ah, block ah,* Footty turned his AK-47 towards the car Big Zeke was behind. *wopwopwopwopwop,* He started chopping at him, the car was bouncing like it had hydraulics built into it. Big Zeke had to get from behind it, that AK-47 was putting holes in the side of that car the size of baseballs. Pooh Bear gave Big Zeke some cover fire, *block ah, block ah, block ah, block ah,boomboomboom boom boom boomboom,rat tat tat tat tat tat tat tat* tat, the shit was going down. Bay Boy tried to make a move, he stood up and ran towards Footty and E-money as they were trying to reload those automatic weapons. *block ah, block ah,block ah,* but then E-money pulled his Glock 9 mm. *bang bang bang bang bang bang,* Bay Boy went down. Footty pulled out his 45, aiming for Bay Boy's head, but Pooh Bear and Big Zeke wouldn't then let him get a shot off. *boomboomboomboomboomboom,block ah, block ah, block ah, block ah, block ah,* they ran over to Bay boy, as Footty and E-money started to retreat, shooting while they were on the run. Pooh Bear and Zeke made it to Bay Boy. Bay Boy was just lying there. Big Zeke thought he was dead, but he just had the wind knocked out of him, the bulletproof vest did its job catching all three bullets. You can hear the police closing in fast. Pooh Bear had a plan for that to. Each of them ran to the van, pulled off their masks, and there long-sleeved-black shirts, and snapped their black pants from the side. See each one of them had a dirt bike in the back of that van. They started them up and was out of there before you knew it. Footty and E-money were still running when a cop car spotted them and gave chase. Footty and E- money split up, but both cops went after E- money because they saw a gun in his hand. E-money was running as fast as he could, but those two cops were on his ass. E-money hopped over a couple of poles, then jumped over a fence, and it still didn't help. The cops radioed in for backup. Then E-money came to a wall, that was too high to get over.

The cops drew their weapons, and said, "freeze motherfucker, put your hands where I can see them, or we will shoot!" E-money stopped running, put his hands up, into the air.

"Now turn around slowly." E-money turned around as slow as he could.

"Now get down on your knees." E-money got down on his knees.

169

One cop said to the other, "We should kill this son of a bitch for making us run."

"Alright, fuck it, let's do it. It ain't nothing but a little paperwork."

Then two shots rang out, as E-money closed his eyes prepared to die, until he opened them and saw both cops laying on the ground, with Footty standing in between them screaming, "Let's go hommie." Then Footty and E-money ran off into the night.

AUTHORS NOTE

Hello, my name is Zeke Lyons, I am the author of forty cal. The legend of BlackJack, I want to thank you for taking interest in my book. I hope you enjoyed it. I know you have a lot of questions that you want answered, and they will be, in the second installment, that will be coming soon, and it is called, forty cal. 2, what's in the dark, shall come to light.

www.ingramcontent.com/pod-product-compliance
Lightning Source LLC
Chambersburg PA
CBHW070033120726
47909CB00003B/1137